Tildie was over ___
Indian camp.

Tildie crossed the last few yards, hurling herself into the white man's arms. Distrustful, Boister shed his wariness and grabbed one of the giant's legs and Mari, the other. Tildie buried her face against his chest. She cried with relief.

It felt right to be in his strong arms. His tall frame provided a bulwark to cling to. Larger, sturdier, safer than any man she could recall, he must have stooped to embrace them. She felt his chin upon her head. She heard him laugh and wondered how it could all be so natural.

Finally embarrassed, she leaned back. He wiped tears from her face with gentle fingertips. The villagers crowded around them, rejoicing as they witnessed what appeared to them a happy reunion. The Indians' smiling faces, their strange words of joy surrounded her. She looked up with bewilderment at the white man.

"I came as soon as I heard you were here," he explained.

"I don't understand."

"These are my friends. I learned their language when I lived with them four winters ago. I wasn't very fluent back then. When I tried to tell them that I didn't want one of their Indian maidens, that my God had chosen a woman for me, they thought I already had a wife, not that I had yet to find her. When you knelt to pray as they'd seen me do, they decided you were my woman. They haven't seen many people kneel to pray.

KATHLEEN PAUL lives in Colorado Springs. Retired from teaching, she gets that weekly dose of kids she needs to keep going by being a storyteller in the Sunday school department of her church. During the week she leads two workshops for Christian writers. Her life is full with an eighty-five-year-old mom in residence to keep her in line, two grown children to keep her active, and three dogs to keep her laughing.

Books by Kathleen Paul

HEARTSONG PRESENTS
HP334—Escape

To See
His Way

Kathleen Paul

Heartsong Presents

In memory of Jan Wayne Paul, a modern adventurer.

A note from the author:
*I love to hear from my readers! You may correspond with me
by writing:* **Kathleen Paul**
Author Relations
PO Box 719
Uhrichsville, OH 44683

ISBN 1-58660-151-2

TO SEE HIS WAY

Cover design by Robyn Martins.

PRINTED IN THE U.S.A.

one

"It's hot, Tildie," Marilyn complained.

"That's the truth, Mari." Tildie reached over to wipe the sweat from the little brown face with an old faded scrap of calico. "You're getting darker, and your hair's getting lighter everyday."

"I want my hair to be blond and curly like yours."

"It not such a blessing as you'd think, Cousin. And I don't turn a golden tan, but rather red—like a ripe tomato."

Marilyn giggled and squeezed her rag doll closer. Her legs hung over the back of the wooden seat and swung merrily. The worn canvas tarp covering the bowed frame of the buckboard provided blessed shade. Even so, the sun blazed in the sky, and they found it more and more difficult to ignore the discomfort of the wind, the heat, and the hard surface they sat upon.

The wagon lurched, and Tildie grabbed both the wooden seat and the shoulder of her littlest cousin, Evelyn, at the same time. How could the little cherub sleep with the sweltering heat and the unmerciful, jostling wagon wheels hitting every rut and ridge in the dirt trail?

The heat of Colorado's summer sun permeated even the interior of their wagon. In the distance, the Rocky Mountains rose majestically, looking as if they could be reached by nightfall. It was an illusion. The lone wagon had many miles to travel before it even reached the foothills. Four days would just bring them to their destination, a fort on the Arkansas River.

The wagon hit a deep rut, and everyone held tight to keep from falling out. Marilyn turned a stormy face to scowl at

5

her stepfather's back. He drove the wagon in a slumped position, growling at the horses from time to time and never speaking to the woman who sat beside him.

Tildie followed her gaze, and her own lips thinned to a stern line. She had not expected the unhappy home she found after traveling to Aunt Matilda's. Maybe she'd made a mistake in coming. She shook her head over her selfishness. It wasn't the ideal situation she'd dreamed of, but she'd found love from the children and felt she helped her despairing aunt.

When she left Indiana, Tildie expected to join the only family she had. The situation in Lafayette was bleak, the memories hard to deal with. She'd been alone and desperate to be within the warm circle of family once more. Unfortunately, the decision to travel west had brought her to an even more unsatisfactory situation.

Aunt Matilda's three little ones perched with Tildie on the wide shelf across the back tailgate of the old buckboard. The wind blew sporadically from the west, and each cloud of dirt kicked up by horses and wagon swirled away before it could settle on the children. Tildie braced herself against the pole that supported the covering. Evelyn's wet little head rested on her lap. The toddler's short, tawny curls clung in tight rings darkened by sweat. Tildie kept a hand on the babe's shoulder for fear a bounce would toss the sleeping child to the hard, stony ground.

Four-year-old Marilyn, called Mari for her sweet, merry temperament, sat as a mirror image across from her grown cousin. The cousins favored each other with the same golden tresses, dark lashes and brows, small even features, and sparkling blue eyes. Once, they had gone to the Breakdon settlement and strangers had assumed Mari was Tildie's little girl. Aunt Matilda didn't care, or perhaps, she didn't even notice. Nothing much penetrated the weary despondency which surrounded the older woman.

Tildie reached across to help Mari arrange her rag doll on

the bench to lay much the way her sister Evelyn laid against Tildie. Mari patted her dolly's shoulder and grinned at her big cousin.

Between the little girls sat Boister, whose real name was Henry. His father had been Aunt Matilda's first husband—a kind and sturdy man who objected to his namesake being called Little Henry and called him Mister. Aunt Matilda laughingly called him Beau. Somehow, Beau and Mister got mixed and slurred together. The resulting "Boister" had been a good appellation for the energetic child full of rambunctious fun before his pa died.

A sudden jolt rocked them, and Tildie grabbed Evelyn into her arms. Marilyn screeched and clung to the seat. Her doll fell into the wagon. Boister fell in as well, but he scrambled back. The normally placid team lurched wildly before the wagon. The horses reared and backed erratically, causing the buckboard to pitch. They flailed their legs in the air and voiced their terror in high pitched whinnies. Masters's rough voice could be heard above the clamor as he fought for control. One last mighty jolt sent the four passengers in back tumbling to the ground. The horses bolted, leaving them in the dust.

"Snake!" Boister's voice cracked.

Tildie's head jerked around as her arms froze in their reach for Mari's still form.

A large, menacing snake coiled by the trail ahead of them. The distinct buzzing of his rattle warned the humans to stay away. He unwound, stretching out to his full five feet. Evidently he'd had enough of the trail, horses, wagons, and humans. He slithered off into the brush, leaving the petrified cousins.

Tildie shuddered at the sight of the snake's rattled tail disappearing under a bush. Closing her eyes, she inhaled deeply to calm herself and whispered, *"Thank you, Lord."*

She dismissed her bruises. The fall had shaken her up but

caused no permanent damage. Boister stood beside her. She handed him the crying Evelyn and crawled over to Mari. The child gasped for air, and Tildie hoped she'd find nothing more seriously wrong other than having the wind knocked out of her. Tildie spoke soothing words to the frightened child as she ran her hands over little arms and legs to feel for broken bones. Finally, the breathing became regular with only hiccuping sobs. Tildie, convinced that the injuries consisted of bumps, bruises, and a scare, rocked Mari gently in her arms.

She peered down the road after the disappearing wagon. Nothing blocked her view. They sat on the grasslands where nothing higher than thimbleweed, spring larkspur, and bristly crowfoot waved above the blue grama grasses. In a short distance the land changed abruptly. But for now, through the cloud of dust, she could see the wagon bouncing wildly behind the runaway team.

The trail rose on an incline. Surely the horses would tire and stop soon. Her assessment of her surroundings transpired in a breath of time.

Boister dumped the other wailing sister in her lap and sat down on a boulder to wait. He scowled after the disappearing wagon. "Didn't want to go to Fort Reynald, anyway," he said.

"Me needer." Marilyn stuck out her lower lip in a childish pout. She squirmed around in Tildie's lap to face her cousin on this very important issue. "I don't want you to marry that man. I want you to stay with us."

"I haven't said I'm going to marry the man your stepfather picked out, but he might be nice." Tildie tried to sound hopeful. In her heart, she knew any associate of John Masters could not be a suitable husband.

"Don't you like being our cousin? Don't you want to stay with us?" asked Marilyn.

Boister snorted. He knew better than to ask those baby questions. Wasn't much any of them could do now that John Masters had made his decision.

His little sister ignored him and persisted in pestering her cousin. "How come you don't have real children?"

"Not my time yet, Mari. And I shall always be your cousin." Tildie planted a kiss on her cousin's damp forehead.

She enjoyed mothering the children. With their own mother lost in a world of despondency, the children had adopted Tildie as the one to run to for everything from a torn sleeve to a hurting splinter.

"God will give me a husband first, then all the little ones I could possibly want." She smiled with more assurance than she felt. John Masters's attempt to interfere with God's order might succeed. Between the two, Tildie would count on God to come out the stronger. It was just that sometimes it was hard to remember when, for all intents and purposes, it sure looked like she was heading down a dusty trail in the hot sun towards a mighty unpleasant future.

She shook her head, turning to God with her perplexing thoughts. *I don't see Your hand in this Lord. Let me have faith in the things I cannot see.*

"If you have babies will they be my sisters?" Mari demanded her attention.

"They'll be your cousins," Tildie answered with a brief smile. Mari's chatter brought up the disturbing picture of a husband she might not like. She'd be sharing her life with a stranger if she wasn't careful. John Masters's schemes could be difficult to thwart, but God was on her side. No one could force her to marry anybody. She could get a job and just stay in Fort Reynald. That would mean being separated from these children, but that was a certainty anyway. John Masters had made it clear she was not welcome on the homestead any longer.

Tildie set Mari and Evie on their feet and scrambled up herself. The wagon had disappeared, clean out of sight. They might as well start walking. Sitting here in the sun with no shade might scorch them clear through. They'd just follow the tracks. Before long they'd be able to spot the wagon lumbering back to get them.

The trail barely distinguished itself from the rough terrain around it. The deep ruts held an overgrowth of thistle, weeds, and porcupine grass. In spite of this, Tildie felt confident that following the wagon was better than waiting in the searing sun.

"Come on, we'll walk to meet them," Tildie said with what cheerfulness she could muster. She looked over at Boister, still slumped on top of his rock. The boy looked too sober. He always looked too sober. He often acted like a grumpy old man instead of a six-year-old boy. He had his reasons, she figured.

Big Henry had died in a rockslide, and Boister had been the first to reach him. The little boy had found his father's large familiar hand sticking out of the rubble and pulled with all his might. It took grown men two hours to remove the boulders that had crushed the life out of Henry Baskerman. Boister had been crushed in spirit, and the somber, haunted look masked a once vital personality. Aunt Matilda's letters had been full of the little pistol's derring-do adventures before the death of her husband. Tildie wondered which was the greater tragedy: losing his father, or acquiring Masters as a stepfather.

Matilda had married John Masters within six months. She couldn't handle adversity and thought John would take the weight of grief off her shoulders. She was mistaken. John Masters proved a burden of grief in himself, and he broke what little courage the widow had left. He acted surly to the children who were not his and later showed no more tolerance of the squalling babe that came out of his own union with Matilda.

The promising spread failed without Henry's energetic enthusiasm for tilling the soil. Masters sold off the cattle to buy whiskey and poker chips. The sparkle of admiration in

Masters's eye as he courted Matilda turned out to be the gleam of greed. When his plans for a life of ease on an already established bit of land failed, he blamed everyone but himself. The children often took the brunt of his wrath.

Tildie tried an encouraging smile and held a hand out to Boister. "Come on. I'm glad you're not still in the wagon. At least we have one strong man to protect us."

Boister shot her a look, not accepting her false dependence on him. He didn't outwardly scorn her puny attempt to make things seem better, but he didn't take the offered hand. He started off without speaking, plodding ahead of the girls and Tildie.

Tildie sighed and took hold of each little girl's hand. So far she hadn't been able to soften Boister's hardened heart. She would just keep trying and praying.

"Look." She pointed to a bird in the dust several yards away from their path. "That's a meadowlark. See his yellow vest and black cravat? Watch him bend over to touch the ground. Doesn't it look like he's bowing?"

They stopped in the trail to watch this strange performance.

"What's he doing?" asked Mari.

"I don't really know, but I've always thought he's hiding. See, his back blends in with the dirt and dry plants. With his yellow front ducked down, he almost disappears."

"You think he thought that out himself?" Boister sounded doubtful.

Tildie laughed. "No, not really. With that little bitty head there must be a little bitty brain within. God gives His creatures an instinct to protect themselves."

"He's not very well hidden," Boister scoffed.

"Sometimes God lets humans laugh at His creatures' funny ways," she continued. "It's all right to laugh. God says He gives us joy."

Boister cast her one of his tolerant looks. He was telling her as clearly as if he had spoken that her nonsense wasn't for him. He marched on.

As they returned to their hot walk, Tildie fell into her own thoughts. She'd been with the children six months. Orphaned in Indiana, she'd written to the aunt she was named after. Her mother's sister lived in southern Colorado territory, near Kansas. Tildie longed to go to the aunt she remembered from her childhood. She didn't get the letter which said *not* to come. She knew it existed, had known since the moment she walked across the wooden porch and knocked on the door. John Masters told her.

"Do you want to marry the grocer?" asked Mari, coming back to the topic which most disturbed her.

Her question startled Tildie.

"I don't know if I do, or I don't," she answered truthfully. "Reckon I'll decide that once I've met this Mr. Armand des Reaux."

"I don't want you to marry him. You'll never get to visit us." Marilyn couldn't quite keep the whine out of her voice.

Tildie closed her eyes and prayed against the pain in her heart. How could she desert these children? Tildie knew what her absence would mean to them. It was she who sang at her chores. She told funny stories as they lay in bed at night. She hugged them, laughed, and said out loud she loved them. Tildie imitated her Aunt Matilda as she had been years ago on an Indiana farm. Tildie had been the happy child. Matilda had been the almost grown playmate.

Now, Tildie's aunt spoke rarely. She never laughed. She walked in a daze through the house. She sat in her rocker while Tildie did the chores. It made Tildie's heart ache to think of her aunt, but a worse pain grabbed her when she considered the life the children would have in that house with John Masters and no one to act as a buffer.

Boister turned around and walked backwards. He'd listened to the three he pretended to ignore. Now he looked from his sister to his cousin. He spoke words to his sister, but his eyes bore a hole in Tildie. "She don't have no reason to want to visit us. *I* wouldn't come visit us."

"Boister," said Tildie earnestly, "if Mr. des Reaux turns out to be an agreeable man, I'll ask him if you and your sisters can stay with me."

"Won't be," Boister stated flatly. "He be a friend of *him*." He jerked his head in the direction the wagon had taken.

The image of John Masters's unkempt, hulking figure towering in rage over her aunt's diminished form sprang up in Tildie's mind. She shuddered. Secretly, she agreed with Boister's estimate of the circumstance.

She'd been praying with all her might since John Masters returned from a trip with news he was getting rid of the extra mouth dumped on him. He told her he got her a husband, a Frenchie who owned his own store at a new fort established by some fur traders. It was close to the foothills of the Rockies on the Arkansas River.

Tildie yearned to see the mountains. She selfishly wanted to escape the atmosphere of oppression in her aunt's home. She liked the idea of being somewhere where people came and went, providing more variety in company than her family, the drunken head of it, and a few cowhands. However, she had no desire to take up residence in a fort where she would very likely be the only white woman. She thought the Mexican and Indian women would be interesting, but she doubted they would speak English. What kind of fellowship could you have with someone you couldn't talk to?

Her fear of traveling in the company of her uncouth uncle disappeared the day he announced the whole family was making the trip. Suspicion replaced her fear. Why would he bother taking everyone? He certainly never put himself out for anyone else's pleasure. The mystery vanished when she heard him tell a silent Aunt Matilda that he'd show her he could provide for her and her brats. The Frenchie would give them clothes and winter supplies when they delivered the bride.

Tildie sighed and her eyes fell on the little boy trudging along a few feet ahead of them. He'd turned back around and stalwartly tramped in the heat. She called after him. "If Mr. des Reaux is impossible, Boister, then I won't marry him, and I'll get a job. It may take time, but you're my family, and someday we'll be together. Maybe Fort Reynald will have places I can work. I worked in a boardinghouse to get the money to come to you."

"You'd better pray about that," said Mari, her little voice echoing the exact tone Tildie often used.

Tildie smiled. She marveled at Marilyn. Mari absorbed the comfort of a loving Father God and the friendship and protection of His Son. Boister believed, too, but so far, the joy of the Lord had not released him from his sorrow. Tildie knew it would, but she was impatient, especially now that it looked like they would be separated. She wouldn't be there to nourish the little ones with the Word of God.

Her faith had provoked this scheme to marry her off. John Masters might grumble about an extra mouth to feed, but his real complaint railed against the Lord Tildie knew so well. She received banishment from her aunt's home because she stood for something which was vinegar and gall to her new uncle. John Masters enjoyed someone else doing the work, and Tildie did plenty. He might have kept her on for that reason, but Tildie's love of God nearly drove him wild.

He had called her every name he could think of. His vocabulary did not extend to fancy words. In his raving, he couldn't quite bring up the high-sounding names he needed to express his disgust. Tildie got the message, though. He thought her sanctimonious, self-righteous, and interfering.

The children loved her and flourished in the sunshine of her faith. She whispered prayers to them in the morning after they stretched, before they threw off the covers. She prayed with them when they ate, got hurt, or lost something. She tucked them in with a prayer. She even sang hymns.

As John Masters's intolerance became louder and more abrasive, Tildie had tried to be less demonstrative in his presence, not wishing to bring on the distressing bouts of fury. But Masters chafed against her quietness, as well.

"I've been praying," Tildie assured her little cousin. "Remember, God listens to your prayers, too. No matter what happens, you must talk to Him."

Marilyn nodded, but Boister who had glanced back at them firmly turned his face to look away.

Troubled, Tildie prayed, *Oh Father, please, I want them with me. I want to reach Boister.*

"Let's pray for God to direct our steps," she said aloud. "Then I'll tell you about some stepping stones back in Lafayette, Indiana, that take you across a little creek to a lush meadow where fireflies blink at the end of day."

"What's fireflies?" asked Mari.

"First, we pray," said Tildie.

two

How could the wagon have gotten so far ahead? Didn't they stop? They couldn't have just gone on. Surely John Masters would turn the wagon and come back for them. After all, she was the cargo he was taking to market.

Tildie and the children trudged up the rocky path. Evie perched on her back, legs wrapped around her waist, arms encircling her neck. Tildie had stopped talking, saving her energy for walking. Sweat beaded on her forehead and trickled into her eyes, making them sting and water. Her legs felt heavy. Muscles protested, both from the fall off the wagon and this abominable trek.

Freshly scarred rocks on the trail marked where the metal rim of the wagon wheel or horse's iron-shod hoof had struck. However, no sight or sound of the wagon itself appeared. Tildie fought an increasing sense of uneasiness.

The terrain had altered considerably as they walked, always trudging uphill. They approached the summit, walking on the twenty foot wide rock and earth shelf. The road dropped off steeply at one side and rose just as abruptly on the other. They kept to the middle, avoiding the cliff-like edge.

A cluster of elm trees offered welcome shade, and they stopped to rest. In spite of the heat, the little girls leaned close to their cousin as she sat against the largest tree trunk. Boister tried to stretch out in a patch of grass a little ways off. The rocks dug into his back and he sat up immediately. Tildie shut her eyes, resting and praying against the unease building in her.

"What's that?" Boister sprang to his feet. "Do you hear it?" He ran towards the top of the rise.

"Boister, wait!" cried Tildie as she scrambled up.

The trail turned abruptly at the top of the ridge. Boister stood gazing over the edge. His little from froze in a rigid attitude. Even before she reached him, she knew by his stance that something horrible lay before him. Tildie wrapped her arms around him and drew him away before she looked herself. When she saw the scene below, she gasped, turning the stiff boy away from the sight and pressing his face against her dress futilely blocking the view.

At the bottom of the steep ravine the wagon lay shattered. One horse lay lifeless. The other horse struggled to rise, then fell still, only to repeat the pathetic attempt a moment later. Halfway down among the rocks sprawled the still figure of Matilda Masters, only recognizable by the color of her dress. A brilliant red stain flowed from her shattered form, across the rocks. Masters was nowhere to be seen.

Boister suddenly wrenched away from her and ran to the other side of the trail. Bending over, he threw up, then crumpled into a sobbing huddle. Tildie scooped him up in her arms. Tears blinded her as she stumbled back down the trail. Mari approached, her hand firmly clasping Evie's. They looked so small and helpless.

Dear God, this can't be! Tildie's anguish turned her to her Heavenly Father. She reached the smaller children and knelt in the dirt, gathering them all as close to her as she could. She and Boister wept, and the little girls joined them, not really knowing why except that something was terribly wrong.

Eventually, the emotional storm subsided. They clung together, weary. Tildie wondered if she would be able to creep down that sheer drop to her aunt's body. What if she were only injured? Could she move her to safety if she was? Were there ropes in the wagon? Surely, she'd seen some. Threads of a plan began to form in her mind. She must do *something*.

A small sound startled her, and she looked up. The children felt her tense, and they, too, looked up from where their heads were buried against her.

"Indians," whispered Mari.

Three stood on the trail, their black, serious eyes studying the children without emotion. Tildie looked over her shoulder, seeking an escape route. Two more of the bronzed men stood about the same distance behind her, and another two on horseback waited at the turn of the trail. Some of the strange men had circles tattooed on their chests. Others had numerous straight lined scars on their arms. One had what looked like a stuffed crow dangling from his waist.

Three men came forward in long easy strides. The oldest passed without a word. The two younger stopped beside Tildie and the huddled children.

"Be calm, children," she whispered. "Remember Jesus is always with us. He will never leave us nor forsake us." Tildie's voice shook, and she tightened her hold on Evie as one of the Indian men reached for her.

The second man put a hand on her shoulder. She looked up into his face. His serene expression waylaid her fear. She saw sympathy in his eyes. Shocked to find an underlying kindness in one she thought of as a savage, Tildie didn't know what to think. He placed his hand under her arm and, with no visible effort, lifted her to her feet.

One Indian took Evelyn who whimpered softly. Tildie saw him pat her back. The second released her arm and swooped up Mari. Mari gasped and terrified little blue eyes peered over the Indian's shoulder as the men started up the hill. Tildie shook herself from her trance, grabbed Boister's hand, and started after them. Wherever they took her girls, she would follow.

Around the bend, several more Indians patiently waited with a group of quiet, unsaddled horses. An Indian efficiently threw Tildie up on a dappled pony. The same Indian hoisted Boister up with another young man. No, not a man, but an adolescent boy. He looked so hard and serious. Tildie gulped down the fear rising in her throat. These people hadn't threatened them. . .perhaps they even meant to help.

As one unit, they started moving. The Indians carrying

Mari and Evie rode on either side of Tildie, so close that her horse needed no guidance from her hand. The men didn't speak. Tildie prayed.

Lord, protect us. Further prayer tumbled through Tildie's bewildered mind. She trembled over words for her unhappy aunt. Her thoughts rambled, mixing with her prayers. Was Aunt Matilda still alive? Where was John Masters? Did the Indians intend to harm them? *God, are You watching out for us? I promised the children that You would. Your Word says You will. Oh God, I'm scared.*

They reached a descending path and turned aside to follow it. At the base, a few of the men separated and headed back. Surely they were going to see about the wagon. Was it possible that they would bring her aunt to her? Could she have survived? Was Masters alive?

Her band picked up speed and Tildie concentrated on staying astride the swift pony. If she fell, she would fall under the other horses' hooves. She began to wish that she rode with one of their Indian captors. *Were* they captors, or were they rescuers? What did these men intend? She had only a hazy knowledge of Indians. Was this one of the ferocious tribes, bloodthirsty and inflamed by revenge? How could she know? They were not exactly friendly, neither did they seem hostile.

Tildie swayed and felt herself slipping. A strong hand steadied her. She looked into the face of the man next to her. The same Indian who had first placed a hand on her shoulder gazed steadily into her eyes. She drew strength from his solemn demeanor. He had saved her from a fall. His face registered no emotion. He released her and turned to watch the way they traveled.

Was this God's answer to her fearful questions? Was this action by the stoic Indian meant to relieve her worries? *God, speak to me. I'm scared!* She looked over at Evelyn, riding with an Indian's strong arm around her little body. A big grin brightened her face as they sped along. Her fair hair, the sweat dried now by the wind, flowed back against the

Indian's dark chest, spreading over the dark tattoos.

Okay, I'll trust, promised Tildie.

❧

The village surprised her. She had not expected the neatly erected tepees, the smell of dinner cooking, or the curious stares of the little children.

When she slid off the pony, her knees buckled. Again, the same silent Indian reached to steady her. The older man spoke, and a woman came forward to guide Tildie and the children into a tepee. The woman gave them water to drink.

Even in her anxious state, Tildie stared in fascination at the inside of the Indian's home. Spaced about four feet apart, the framework of twenty-one pine poles made a twenty-foot circle. About two-and-a-half inches in diameter at the base, the poles tapered off as they extended their twenty foot length. The thinner tops rested together as they crossed in a narrow bunch where a hole in the hide covering had a small flap. A shallow hole dug in the middle of the earthen floor smoldered with a small fire. A larger fire had been directly outside the tepee. Bedding, buffalo robes, and various household items were piled in neat order around the sides.

An Indian woman bathed little Evie and chattered to the child in soothing, incomprehensible syllables. An older woman with long braids heavy with gray hair brought water, soothing potions, and a change of clothes. When Tildie and the children were physically more comfortable, the older woman brought them food.

Tildie thanked her. Then, she and the children joined hands to pray. They must have been a strange sight, sitting cross-legged in an Indian tepee, wearing Indian clothing, but praying as they did around the kitchen table of the wooden house on the homestead. The Indian woman watched with serious eyes. When they finished praying and began to eat, she gave a decisive nod as if she understood something from the little scene. She abruptly walked out of the tepee.

Left alone, Tildie and the children relaxed and enjoyed the

surprisingly tasty stew.

"When are we going home?" Mari asked. With her hunger satisfied, she had thoughts of something besides her stomach.

"I don't know," answered Tildie. Evie curled up in her lap. The long dusk of summer finally deepened into night. The wind stilled as it often did at twilight and insects tuned up just as they did back home. Evie hugged Tildie and seemed almost content.

Boister cast her a worried look, and Tildie started speaking quickly for fear he would say something upsetting to the girls. He was perfectly capable of predicting their death by some means of torture. "They've been very nice to us, haven't they? I wonder if any of them speak English."

"Is Mama dead?" asked Mari.

Tildie looked at her small, sad face and longed for a better answer. "I think so," was all she could say.

"Did she go to heaven?" Mari asked solemnly.

"Yes."

"Then she's dead, Tildie. She wouldn't go to heaven unless Jesus called her. Jesus called Pa. Now he's called Mama. She'll be happy, Tildie, don't worry."

Tildie stared at her little cousin. She hadn't told the children these things. Apparently, before their mother withdrew into her shell of despair, she had talked to them of God and heaven. Tildie nodded, "That's right, Mari. Your ma and pa are in heaven."

"He isn't," said Boister. Clearly the response indicted John Masters. Boister never referred to the man by any name if he could help it.

The boy's cold expression clutched at her heart. Remembering his tears at the scene of the accident, Tildie sighed. Perhaps those tears signified something good. Boister so very rarely showed emotion. The apathetic attitude resembled his mother's too much. A shiver ran down Tildie's spine in spite of the warmth of the night air.

She bowed her head, closed her eyes, and rested her cheek

against Evie's curly head. *God, this is too much for me. I can't take care of these children. Boister hurts so badly. Inside, he's hurt. I don't know what to say or do. Are we going to die here? Will I be able to keep little Evie, Mari, and Boister if we get out? Where will we live? How will I provide for them? Oh, God, this is impossible. You must truly be able to achieve the impossible this time. I have no choice but to leave it all in Your hands.*

Evie gave a soft muzzled snore in her sleep, and Tildie gently placed her on a mat next to the buffalo skin wall. Marilyn took her place in Tildie's lap, and even Boister scooted closer. Tildie sang softly. She wandered through the tunes without any order. Sometimes she sang one through, and others, she skipped from verse to verse, using the words of the old hymns to soothe her own heart as well as the children's.

Horses came into the camp. Voices murmured in low urgent tones. Even knowing that she could not understand, Tildie strained to hear the words. Finally, she heard a shifting of feet and horses being led away. The older Indian woman came into the tepee. She handed Mari's rag doll to her. To Tildie, she handed Aunt Matilda's Bible.

"Thank you, thank you," Tildie said through the tears, clutching the precious Book.

Some of the Indians had been to the wagon. They'd brought these items to her. In light of the language barrier, questions were futile. Tildie looked at the old woman and saw understanding and compassion in her face. Tildie gratefully accepted the comfort God sent for this moment.

ૐ

The old Indian woman apparently lived alone in the tepee. She made no attempt to verbally communicate with her guests. With kind eyes and firm nudges, she prodded the newcomers into doing what she wanted. The first day, she showed them how to help with the chores, beginning with building up the fire for their cooking. None of the village Indians seemed to be much interested in the little family and let the old woman be in charge of all their doings.

"Couldn't we just leave?" asked Boister at midday.

"I'm too sore to walk very far," answered Tildie. "And I don't know where we are, or where we should go."

"We should head for the mountains. That's the way we were headed before. Or we could turn away and keep the mountains to our backs. That's the way to go home," Boister said, then fell silent.

A horrible prospect crossed Tildie's mind, and she hastened to say something that would keep Boister from striking out on his own in some attempt to find help. "We should stay together, Boister. I need you to help me be brave. I mean it. God will send us help or show us how to get back home. Meanwhile, we *must* take care of each other."

Boister nodded, and Tildie took a measure of comfort from the small gesture.

"Who's that old lady?" Mari pointed to the Indian woman who cared for them. "Is she the tribe's grandma?"

"I don't know who she is, Mari, but we should be grateful she's kind to us."

"What should I call her?" asked the little girl with big eyes.

"Older One," said Boister promptly. "If you look around the camp, you won't see anyone older. She has more wrinkles on her face than any I ever saw anywhere."

"The others seem to treat her with a great deal of respect," said Tildie. "Until we learn her name, I guess it would be all right to call her Older One."

๛

Late in the day, more Indians arrived. At the far side of the village, Tildie saw them surrounded by her new neighbors. Through the crowd, she got glimpses of the newcomers. The Indians who had just arrived had a litter with an injured man strapped to it. Older One went over to the crowd, speaking to first one, and then another of her tribe. She waved them impatiently away from her tepee. She obviously did not want the man in addition to her other white guests.

The Indians brought the litter closer, carrying it past Older One's tepee. Tildie gasped as she recognized John Masters's clothing more than his bloody features. She followed the men. The children also started after them, but Older One would not allow it. She turned them back sternly.

The grim Indians placed John Masters in a tepee quite a distance from Older One's. They put him down gently, spoke not a word, and left the tepee quickly. One man stayed to cradle Masters's head and dribble water between his battered lips. Tildie did not think her aunt's husband even swallowed. The Indian stood and walked out.

Tildie knelt beside Masters and looked him over. Dried blood caked one side of his face. His swollen, discolored features bloated with bruises. Loosening the binds which held him to the litter, she saw his broken legs. One mangled hand lay tied with a cloth to stop the bleeding. His raspy breathing pushed a trickle of bloody drool from his mouth. His wounds were too massive for Tildie's few nursing skills. She wondered if even a doctor could save him.

The tepee flap drew back, and an Indian elder walked in. Tildie moved aside as the man knelt beside John Masters, assessing his wounds in a thorough manner. If there were a healer in the village, Tildie felt sure this was the man.

He sat back on his heels and studied the patient in silence. In the end, he stood and walked out without doing anything to aid the wounded man.

Tildie bathed Masters's face and squeezed water into his mouth as she had seen the first Indian do. After some time, another Indian came into the tepee and indicated she must leave. Tildie left feeling inadequate. John Masters was going to die.

three

During the night, Tildie worried. The children snuggled beside her in the pile of animal skins which served as their bed. Older One snored softly from across the way. The stars twinkled through the hole at the top of the tepee where poles crossed and smoke could drift out. Her prayers seemed to go around in circles rising no higher than the little opening to the sky visible above her. The worry weighed them down.

It all boiled down to whether or not she could trust the almighty God who had given her work when her parents and brother died, guided her to Aunt Matilda's home, and given her strength to put up with John Masters's taunts. God had stood close in times of trouble before, but now He seemed distant. Present troubles cast menacing shadows so that she could not see Him. Reason told her that her thinking was faulty, but fear told her there was no help, no end to this predicament. Sleep came eventually, without her soul settling into peace.

❧

The morning surprised Tildie. It mocked her with cheerfulness. Older One chanted a sing-song melody. Birds twittered in the trees. The bustle of the Indian camp echoed the busy noises she had heard the previous morning. Evie chattered her toddler nonsense to the doll Older One had made for her. Mari hurried to help stir the pot of mash. Boister followed another lad down to the stream.

Surely there should be some sign that a man had died, or lay dying. Tildie's eyes turned to the tepee harboring John Masters. Had he made it through the night? She started toward the tepee, but Older One turned her back, just as she

25

had turned the children back the day before. Older One put a bowl before her, and Tildie knew she was to grind the corn. She sighed and sat down in the shade of a tree. As her hands worked the round grinding stone across the rough stone bowl, her mind kept returning to the injured man in the tepee.

After several tries, Tildie escaped Older One's interference and reached the tepee where John Masters lay. She went in cautiously. An old woman sat in the gloomy space and nodded solemnly at her entrance. She did not, however, offer anything more than the acknowledgement of her presence. Tildie knelt beside the broken man.

"John," she spoke after a moment. "John, do you hear me?"

He groaned and stirred slightly.

Contradictory feelings overwhelmed her. This despicable man had caused so much misery. She'd tried not to hate him, but now that he lay helpless before her she realized how great her anger and resentment had grown. She blamed him for taking over her uncle's home and making it a place full of strife. She blamed him for her loving aunt's withdrawal and neglect of the children. She blamed him for every uncomfortable moment she had experienced since she arrived, uninvited, on his doorstep. She even blamed him that they were prisoners in this Indian village. This accusation skittered around the fact that she didn't really believe they were prisoners.

Still, John Masters was despicable, and that was his own fault. He was hateful, proud, a bully, and a lazy, foul-smelling vermin. He deserved to die, and she knew he would go to hell. She looked at the miserable shell that struggled to breathe, sweated with fever, and smelled of death. Her emotions battered against the cold hatred she felt for him. The careful reserve she had used to deal with this man crumbled, and she cried.

"John, can you hear me?"

"Curse you, girl," he muttered. "Nobody asked you to come."

"John, you're going to die," she sobbed. "Aunt Matilda is already dead."

His eyes opened and he looked at her, really looked at her. She knew he saw her and his mind was clear.

"You're going to die, John, and you are the lowest man I have ever met. I'm sure there's someone out there worse than you, but I never met him. You took advantage of a widow's grief. You stole her homestead and ran it down to nothing. You treated her badly, you treated her kids badly, and you even treated your own little girl badly. You're scum."

"Thought you was all goodness," John protested with just a touch of irony in his whispery voice. "Ain't right to talk to a dying man like that."

"You're going to go to hell."

"Reckon so," he gasped.

"You don't have to," she whispered.

"You gonna preach?" The scornful twist to his lips reminded Tildie how often he'd belittled her faith. Still, she was compelled to speak.

"Aren't you scared? Aren't you ashamed? How can you die and face God, knowing He's going to toss you in hell? It's not make-believe or women's talk, John. You're going to find out too late that all the religion you've been scoffing at is true."

Tildie wiped the back of her hand across her eyes, not knowing why she even stayed beside this worthless man who had caused her nothing but grief, who had been the ruin of her aunt's family.

"Too late," his voice bubbled as he repeated the phrase. A trickle of blood oozed out of the corner of his mouth.

"It's not," said Tildie firmly. "You're still breathing. Just admit you're bad and ask for forgiveness. Christ died for you—even you. You can go to heaven if you just say it."

Tildie clenched her fists in her lap. Tears ran down her cheeks, and she no longer tried to stop their flow. He looked at her again. A searching look, but she couldn't meet his eyes. She crossed her arms over her middle, and rocked back and forth as she sobbed.

She saw his eyes close and watched him through blurry vision. His lips moved but no sound came out. He coughed. He seemed unconscious, then his lips moved again. His hand moved toward her, but she cringed away, and it fell limp by his side.

Tildie angrily wiped the tears from her face. She did not want to cry for this man. She took deep breaths, trying to stop this ridiculous emotional outburst. Why was she bawling over this reprobate? She hated him. She felt glad he was dying. She screwed her eyes shut and willed herself to stop, holding her breath and tensing every muscle in her body. She tried to call out to God and found there were no words. *Pray for me, Holy Spirit,* she demanded. *I can't. I can't.*

At last peace descended on her. With slow, calming breaths she returned to her surroundings and opened her eyes to look down on John Masters's face. He was dead, and in his death, the perpetual sneer that had marred his features vanished. He looked calm, at peace.

As she looked at his face, she knew. He had taken Christ as his Savior at the last possible moment. He wasn't going to be punished for all the pain he'd inflicted on Aunt Matilda and the children. He'd escaped punishment. He'd cheated. That's what she felt, even though her mind told her she was wrong to feel that way. God had chosen to be merciful to another wretched sinner.

Tildie rose to her feet and turned away. God was good. His ways were right. She should be happy. Instead, she felt cold and alone.

four

In the weeks that followed, Tildie wondered what they did with his body. As far as she could tell, it just disappeared the next day.

The Indians' way of expressing their condolences left her confused. They did not speak to her or show any sympathy, yet she sensed they knew of her loss and respected her grief.

In her unsettled state of emotions, it was a good thing that they could not exchange comments. From time to time she found herself crying. How could she have explained that she cried for her aunt, not John Masters? She cried because she had never gotten to visit with the aunt she remembered from her youth. That woman was destroyed by the time she reached Colorado.

She cried because she was angry with herself for the bitter feelings she had about John Masters's salvation. She cried because she was afraid. She was hounded by the responsibility of caring for her little cousins. She feared being among the Indians, even in the face of Older One's kindness. She feared going back to the white settlement where the good citizens would undoubtedly want to take the children from her and place them in homes where they could be cared for. She cried because those good citizens were probably right; she wouldn't be able to provide for the children adequately.

She cried because, in all of this, she should have depended on God and been strong in her faith. Instead, she slipped away from the children so she could cry without alarming them or cried quietly in the night, thinking no one would know.

When her parents and brother had died, the pastor and church members bolstered her faith. On her own, she apparently had no perseverance. Fear dogged her every waking moment, and this disappointed her. Surely she could be strong in the Lord through adversity. When she analyzed her situation, she carefully counted her blessings. She and the children were housed, fed, and treated well. Yet, she dwelled on what might happen and could not turn her mind as she should to think of things that were good and lovely. It was only through a conscious effort to turn everything over to God in prayer that she kept her sanity. Gradually, the turmoil subsided and the routines of life filled the great inner void.

Mari and Boister began to understand the Indians and spoke words of their language. Tildie made very little progress and had to laugh each time Older One threw up her hands in despair over her stupidity. The impatient Indian hostess would haul one of the children over to Tildie's side, speak to Boister or Mari, then wait for the child to translate. Her expression clearly indicated that she thought the mother was the slowest of the white guests in her tepee.

The days lengthened, and Tildie began to notice the individuals in the Indian village. A young Indian boy, White Feather, took Boister under his wing. They went out together, and although Tildie had trepidation over just where they went and what they did, they came back, dirty and content. Boister learned to fish and hunt with the help of his new friend. Mari played with the other little girls, but she also spent time doing chores for Older One. Little Evie toddled among the women and children and gathered the same tolerant affection as the other toddlers of the tribe.

Slowly, Tildie became aware of one Indian who watched her. This strong young man often stood close by. His serious face held dark, piercing eyes, following her every movement. When he came close to the tepee, Older One scolded him and shooed him away. Once she pushed Tildie into the tepee and would not let her come back out until the men rode off from camp.

This new worry occupied Tildie's mind. Obviously, the man thought a young white woman would make a good wife. Tildie began to think less of her confused grief over the deaths of Matilda and John Masters and began to concentrate on what went on around her. She had no desire to be claimed by this Indian. She stayed closer to Older One or with a group of the other Indian women.

Older One showed Tildie how to cut fresh venison into strips and lay it out to dry in the sun. Tildie's hands ached from the hours of tedious labor. As in many cases before, she found herself admiring the older woman for her skill and stamina. No stranger to hard work herself, she marveled how these Indian women worked endlessly. They laughed, as well. Often running chatter between the ladies merrily lightened their mood as they diligently repeated a monotonous chore. Listening to the rhythm of their talk, Tildie could almost imagine her white neighbors in Lafayette sitting around a quilting frame, exchanging the same peaceful banter.

❧

The day had been long. Tildie took off her work dress and put on another Older One provided. She carried the soiled dress down to the creek along with several other items that Older One thrust into her arms. Tildie enjoyed this one chore. In the shade of an elm tree, she sat on the outcrop of flat rock, dangling her feet in the water as she scrubbed the clothes in the gently flowing stream. Mari and Evie had tagged along behind her, and they played by the water's edge.

Just as the thought crossed her mind that Boister was turning into a little fish from his daily swims with his friend, she heard a splash. Evie floundered in shallow, slow-moving water. Mari gave a cry of alarm and jumped in after her. Tildie tossed aside the shirt she held and scrambled down the bank. With a leap and two strides through the cold water, she had hold of Mari, but Evie moved beyond her reach. Tildie turned quickly and shoved the older child toward the shore, urging her to climb out. Frantic, Tildie swung back to catch Evie only to see the child doing a fair dog paddle. Unfortunately, she paddled away from Tildie and the bank.

"Evie, come back!" cried Tildie. She hurried after her, but the smooth rocks in the stream bed turned under her feet. With each slip, her little cousin got farther away.

A splash downstream alerted Tildie to the presence of the solemn Indian who shadowed her in camp. He stood in the path of the oncoming child and scooped her into his arms. With confident strides, he came upstream. Evie clung happily to her rescuer. The Indian reached Tildie and put a hand under her arm to steady her as they made their way to the bank.

Dancing and clapping, Mari laughed at them. The Indian put Evie down next to her sister and helped Tildie up the slight incline. Tildie hugged the children and laughed with them, grateful that nothing serious had befallen them. She stood up, wringing the water from the skirt of her Indian gown and shyly looked up at their rescuer.

He stood watching, a glimmer of humor brightening his eyes and bringing a softness to his normally aloof expression. Tildie had learned that these Indians had a well-developed sense of humor, even to the point of some very uproarious practical jokes. She smiled at him, recognizing that he, too, found the escapade amusing.

"Thank you," Tildie said. His expression sobered, and he looked deep into her eyes. She turned away. Tildie had no desire to offend the man, but his gaze was warm and too intimate. His interest frightened her.

"Thank you," she said again, quickly picking up the laundry.

"Come, girls," she commanded. "We must get you out of those wet clothes."

"We'll dry," Mari pointed out.

"Come," she answered abruptly and hurried towards camp. Mari helped Evie up and took hold of her chubby hand. The girls gave the Indian one more parting grin. They'd enjoyed the dunking and hastened after Tildie only because they were accustomed to obeying.

That night as Tildie lay in bed with her three cousins, she prayed in earnest—something that had been hard since John Marshall's death.

Thank You, Father, for keeping Mari and Evie safe. Forgive me for being such a weakling. I am trying to trust You. I know that You will provide for us. I admit I'm afraid of just how You'll provide, but I trust You. I'll try not to be such a coward. I'll try not to demand things my way. But, please, Father, let us stay together. Please, let us be a family. Please, don't take the little ones from me. I trust You. I trust You. I want to trust You.

Morning came with the usual tasks Tildie had learned to expect. She was stirring a pot when a shadow fell across her, and she looked up to see an elder with the Indian who followed her standing at his shoulder. She quickly rose and faced them.

The elder looked her over and nodded his approval.

"You need a man," he stated flatly, surprising her by speaking English.

Oh God, give me the right words. I must answer carefully.

Assurance came to her. She did not need a man. As a child of God, she was in His care. Even though her faith had been weak of late, she knew that His care was far superior to the care of any man.

Confidently she shook her head and spoke softly. "No, I have Someone."

The older man turned and spoke briefly to the younger Indian. They walked away, leaving Tildie relieved that it had taken so little to turn them from their purpose.

five

Tildie looked up as the other women began to stand and prattle. She followed a pointing finger to a giant white man striding into the village beside an Indian.

A Swede, thought Tildie immediately as she observed him. *No other race towers over others in that golden aura like the Swedish people back home in Indiana.*

A large, reddish-gold dog followed the two travelers. The dog had a peculiar backpack, carrying part of the load for his master.

The white man smiled easily as he exchanged greetings with many of the tribe. Several children dashed out to pet the dog, exclaiming happily as they trotted beside the two men and the dog.

Tildie had never seen a man so stunning. His straight blond hair hung down over his collar. With a healthy tan, he was still fair beside the swarthy Indians. Straight nose, firm lips, and squarish chin, he was handsome. His expression radiated warmth. His light-colored eyes smiled on those around him. Dressed in buckskins and homespun cloth, with dark leather boots nearly to his knees, he looked magnificent.

Tildie started walking toward him, vaguely thinking that this was a white man, and a white man would surely speak English. He would help her and the children. She caught Evie up in her arms as she passed and reached out to take Mari's hand to pull her along. By the time he reached the chief's tepee, she'd broken into a run.

Something one of the Indians said drew his attention to her. He turned, watching her. She came to a halt, suddenly unsure. Her eyes searched his. Would this stranger help?

Could he get them out of the Indian village? He smiled, and she recognized the smile.

Odd, but her brother had had just that kind of smile, thin lips which tilted into a crooked smile, full of charm and good humor. Tildie felt as if her own brother had come to rescue her. She ran again as fast as she could, encumbered by the little girls. The crowd of Indians to one side parted, allowing Boister to join her. He ran, too.

Tildie crossed the last few yards, hurling herself into the white man's arms. Distrustful, Boister shed his wariness and grabbed one of the giant's legs and Mari, the other. Tildie buried her face against his chest. She cried with relief.

It felt right to be in his strong arms. His tall frame provided a bulwark to cling to. Larger, sturdier, safer than any man she could recall, he must have stooped to embrace them. She felt his chin upon her head. She heard him laugh and wondered how it could all be so natural.

Finally embarrassed, she leaned back. He wiped tears from her face with gentle fingertips. The villagers crowded around them, rejoicing as they witnessed what appeared to them a happy reunion. The Indians' smiling faces, their strange words of joy surrounded her. She looked up with bewilderment at the white man.

"I came as soon as I heard you were here," he explained.

"I don't understand."

"These are my friends. I learned their language when I lived with them four winters ago. I wasn't very fluent back then. When I tried to tell them that I didn't want one of their Indian maidens, that my God had chosen a woman for me, they thought I already had a wife, not that I was waiting to find her. When you knelt to pray as they'd seen me do, they decided you were my woman. They haven't seen many people kneel to pray.

"My name is Jan Borjesson. You have a boy named Boister?" At her nod, he continued. "They decided he's my son because the names sound alike. That would make sense to them. Moving Waters came to my cabin with the wonderful news that my woman had arrived from the East."

Tildie's head went down. She couldn't look the handsome stranger in the face. She stared at his feet and felt herself blushing. She knew it wasn't a delicate flush, but a searing red, covering her neck and cheeks. She could feel the warmth of her embarrassment and was embarrassed even more by the rosy betrayal of her emotions. The stranger, Jan Borjesson, squeezed her shoulders and laughed.

"I'm a missionary, and I'll get you and your children out of here. We'll talk later about where you want to go. Now, I must sit with the elders of the tribe and talk. They'll probably want me to stay a few days to tell them stories from the Book, then I'll take you to the nearest white settlement. Take your children back to your tepee." He gave her a little shake at the same time using a finger to raise her chin. She had to look at him. "Everything is going to be all right."

He smiled, and Tildie felt that everything would, indeed, be all right. She thanked God as she herded the children away from the center of the village.

"Who is he?" asked Boister.

"Could you call him Pa till we get out of here, Boister?" Tildie asked. She knew he'd been listening so that he really knew as much as she did. The important thing was to aid the stranger in their release from the Indians. Surely the Indians would let the little family go peacefully. They'd never shown any hostility towards her or the children.

Boister looked over his shoulder and studied the white man. He stood taller than the tallest of the warriors.

Boister's solemn face reflected the seriousness of his thoughts. He'd never given John Masters the privilege of being called Pa. This stranger had done nothing to deserve the honor. He looked up at Tildie's expectant face.

"If you do, the little ones will," she explained. "It'll make it easier for the Indians to let us go."

"He's going to take us away?" he asked.

Tildie nodded. "Back to a white settlement."

Boister looked down at the dirt, studying his scuffed moccasins. He shrugged. "Guess so," he said and started moving towards Older One's tepee.

They ate supper with Older One while the white man, Jan Borjesson, stayed with his Indian friends. Tildie hoped to talk to him soon. She sat brooding over her bowl of venison stew. Was this missionary an answer to her sporadic prayers? Had God honored her with this blessed rescue even when she had displayed so little faith? Humbly, Tildie prayed her thanks. God again demonstrated His grace, for surely she was not worthy of this delivery. Knowing God loved her even in her weakness spread warmth through Tildie's heart.

In contrast to Tildie's pensive mood, Older One rejoiced. She grinned at Tildie until Tildie realized what the old woman was thinking and blushed. Older One patted her shoulder and looked into her eyes with such a knowing expression that Tildie blushed again. Each time her eyes met the old woman's, Tildie felt her cheeks grow warm. Each blush set Older One off in a cackling giggle.

The fire died down. The children slept in their bed. Older One brought in a new dress of soft, smooth leather for Tildie to wear. The eager Indian woman combed and braided Tildie's blond locks, all the time whispering in her native language words which Tildie could only guess referred to the time when the blond giant would come to the tepee. Older One's grins and chortling heightened Tildie's embarrassment.

Tildie ignored Older One, but still she grew impatient for the Swede to come. She wanted information—when they would leave and where he would take them.

At last Older One snored softly. The tepee flap pulled back and Jan Borjesson's huge form blocked the moonlight.

"Are you asleep?" he whispered.

"No," Tildie answered, just as quietly.

He extended his hand. "Come and walk with me."

Tildie rose from the pallet, crossed the small space, and took his hand naturally. His large dog greeted her, and she dropped the man's hand to pet behind the dog's soft ears.

"Her name is Gladys," offered Jan.

"Gladys?" The oddly proper name for a furry beast startled a nervous giggle out of her.

Borjesson nodded his head, smiling down at her with the crooked grin that made him look so like her brother.

"After a schoolteacher from my youth. I was madly in love with her through two and a half grades. She married the blacksmith."

Tildie looked up at him shyly, wondering if he was teasing her. His face gave nothing away.

They walked through the quiet Indian village. No matter what time of night, there always seemed to be a few Indians awake and watchful. Borjesson nodded to them as they passed, and they returned his nonverbal greeting with grunts and grins. Tildie suspected she knew what they were thinking, and again, she blushed. Perhaps in the moonlight, that telltale red stain would not be noticed by her companion.

At last he indicated they could stop. He offered a seat on a smooth boulder. Gladys sat beside Tildie and rested her chin in her lap. When Tildie did not take the hint, the dog nudged her hand indicating she would gladly accept a good rub behind the ears.

"S'pose you could tell me your name?" asked Jan. "I can't exactly call you, 'wife.' "

"Tildie, Matilda Harris."

"Well, Matilda Harris, you must tell me how best to help you. Where do you wish to go? Where are your people?"

"I have none. I don't know where to go."

"Who were the couple who died in the accident?" He then explained, "My friends have given me a full account of how they found you."

"My aunt and her husband," she answered readily. "They were taking me to Fort Reynald to marry a grocer named Armand des Reaux."

The tall man turned abruptly toward her, "You're to marry des Reaux?" A note of disbelief sharpened his tone.

"I've never met him," she hurried to explain. "My aunt's husband arranged the marriage. John Masters said he couldn't afford to keep me."

"Well, you must certainly *not* go to Fort Reynald. Des Reaux is a mean, uncouth character. We'll just cross that off your list of possibilities." He sat quietly for a moment. "You say your aunt's husband, not your uncle. Why is that?"

"I came out from Lafayette, Indiana, after the last of my family died. I didn't realize my aunt's second husband would be so different from Uncle Henry. I remembered him as generous and warmhearted. They lived near us when I was small.

"At the time it seemed a wise move, and even though the last six months have been difficult, I believe I helped my aunt some and made parts of her life more bearable."

"Are there relatives from the other side of the children's family?"

Tildie shook her head. "It's just me and the three children now."

Tildie looked away trying to hide her discomfort. She realized this gentle giant thought the children were her own. She didn't ordinarily lie to someone who'd been kind to her. The blatant falsehood made her tense. Her parents had trained deceit out of her as any Christian parents would. She must tell him the truth, yet she feared he'd then devise some plan for their well-being which would mean separating them all.

Her conscience battled against her fears. Emotionally, she clung to the reasoning that the circumstances justified the lie. Adding to her guilt, his next words proved he wasn't comfortable with lying, either.

"I'll have to consider this, Tildie." He spoke slowly, "I've never lied to these people. I worked hard to gain their trust. I don't like pretending that we're man and wife, and I would have put an end to it immediately except for a warning from Moving Waters. He believes you're my woman and he hurried me here because Bear Standing Tall wants you for his own."

Tildie nodded. "I know which one that must be." She thought of the man who followed her and helped her with the girls when they fell into the stream.

"Fighting for the right to take you to your own people didn't seem wise. Identified as my woman, you're free to go with me."

She nodded again. So, he was hedging in order to prevent an unpleasant circumstance as well. Somehow, that thought did little to alleviate her own burdened conscience.

"I can take you and the children out of here," Jan continued, "but I'm not sure where to take you. They would think it most peculiar if I just took you to a nearby town and dumped you."

"Would they know?"

"Ah, yes, they would know. They are an astute people, and this is their country. They are very aware of all the white men's movements."

"How do they explain the three children when you have been in this area for over four years?"

"I travel a lot. Gladys and I have explored thousands of miles. I've often been beyond their territory."

At the mention of her name, Gladys left Tildie's side to sit at her master's feet. Jan affectionately petted her, and Tildie noticed for the first time the heavy frosting of white hair around the dog's muzzle. Man and dog had been companions for a long time. This man knew the country, the Indians, the way of the land. She must trust him, putting their lives in his hand and trusting that this is what her heavenly Father desired.

"What do you think we should do about leaving here?" she asked.

"First, I'll take you to my cabin. I need to do a few things to leave it for the winter. Then, I'll take you back to Kansas City. From there you should be able to travel back East."

"There's nothing there for us. The children have, I mean, my aunt has. . .had, a ranch in Colorado close to the Kansas and Texas borders. The land would be ours now. We're the only relatives."

"You wish to return there?"

"Yes, I think so."

"A woman with three children, running a ranch alone. Forgive me, but it doesn't sound very practical."

"A woman with three children returning East to no home, with no money or friends *does* sound practical?"

He grinned. In the moonlight, his teeth shone in that crooked smile. She waited.

He shook his head slowly.

"I don't have an answer for that one. Can you give me twenty-four hours?"

"I don't see that there is a point to it. You may try to make up a reason to dissuade me, but the fact is if God is going to introduce more trials in my life, I'd rather be tried in a place familiar to me than tried in a strange place among strangers."

"You have friends at the ranch?"

"I lived there for six months before John Masters decided to take me to Fort Reynald."

He was quiet for a moment, looking up to the stars. When he finally spoke, the question startled her. "What happened to your husband?"

"I've never had a husband, Mr. Borjesson."

He turned to look at her then. Although she hadn't planned to tell him, she was relieved that she had. The deception had made her uneasy, and she knew that God would honor truth.

"I'm only eighteen. I would have had to marry when I was eleven to be Boister's mother." Tildie smiled as she saw his face in the moonlight. His expression held no hint of condemnation. "The children are my aunt's. The Indians assumed they were mine."

"This does get more complicated, doesn't it?" The missionary smiled, and she noticed the crinkle lines around his eyes. She was glad she'd told the truth. She nodded, waiting to see what he would say.

"Well, there's no sense making plans without prayer and a good night's sleep. God will make the path clear if we don't rush it. Are you content with that?"

"Yes."

"I'm still here to help you. Do you trust me?"

"As long as you don't try to separate me from the children or the children from each other."

"Now, why would I try to do that?"

"Because it's more practical?"

"I don't see that tearing a family apart would be God's way."

Overwhelming relief flooded through Tildie. She grabbed the giant around the waist and hugged him.

"Thank you. Thank you."

He laughed and awkwardly patted her on the back. "I haven't done anything yet."

six

Jan contentedly sat with the men and told them stories from the Good Book. It pleased him that the Indians asked questions about the great God who cared for all people. He referred to what Paul said in Acts about the Unknown God, stressing that even if God were unknown to a tribe, that did not mean He did not exist.

In the evening, the people of the village gathered around the fire, and he preached to the women and children as well as the men. The custom of the Indians was to relate their stories with a rhythm. There was a cadence of speech reserved just for the great stories of old. Jan, while living with the Indians, had cultivated this method of delivery into his own style. Now he spoke not only in their native tongue, but with the same inflection and flow of their traditional stories.

Jan talked with the medicine man who had been hostile to his words on previous visits. In their legends, the Arapaho people revered a being called Creator who made earth. The old man showed interest in the Bible stories as he had never done before. Jan prayed that his Indian friend would truly hear the Gospel message.

"Tell me if the creator of my people will die if I turn to your God," said the old man as he sat with the missionary in the evening.

"I don't believe that is the way it is." Jan replied earnestly. "You are a man who has always sought the truth. You have spoken to the one you call Creator whom you believe to have power over man and the world. I say that you have talked to God but did not know His name or the things He has revealed to us through His Son.

43

"When you spoke to the Creator of Rain, you were speaking to Jehovah, because He is the God of Rain. When you spoke to the Creator of Light, you were speaking to Jehovah, because He not only is the God of Light, but He created light, and the Book says He *is* Light. You have often spoken to the Creator, but now He has sent me to tell you that there is but one God, the one and only, true and living Jehovah."

"And the evil spirits?"

"There is no God but the good and just Jehovah. Evil spirits would like us to believe that they have the power of God, but they do not. They have the power of fear. In God there is no darkness at all. God does not give us a spirit of fear, but of love, truth, and a sound mind. God casts out all fear."

"I will think on these things, Jan Borjesson," the man promised. Jan prayed that he would also remember what he had told him about the purpose of God's Son's journey to the people of the earth.

Another time he told the man, "God is fair. He does not want His people to be ignorant of Him. He sends someone to tell what He has revealed to others. If you were to walk for a hundred years, you would come near the land where His Son visited the earth." He drew a small circle in the dirt and pointed to it as he spoke. "God did not want just these people so far away to possess the great knowledge of Him. He sent people out, here and here and here." Jan drew more rings around the first circle. "These people were told about God. Then, more people went out at God's command to tell of His greatness."

Jan drew more rings around the original.

"You see the Truth of God is spreading." He drew the circles farther and farther away from the center. "Now, I am here," he said, pointing to the outermost circle. "It is because God wants the Arapaho to know."

"It is like a pebble dropped in the pond," said the old medicine man solemnly.

"Yes," said Jan, knowing that it was often best to let the

Indian think rather than to continue talking. After a few moments, the old man nodded, rose to his feet, and left Jan to wonder how much the man believed.

≈

Three days after Jan had walked into the village, he left with his newly acquired "family." They had little to carry as they set out on foot. Rolled blankets held meager supplies. Each carried a bundle and the Indian equivalent to a canteen. Gladys had her saddlebag pouches packed.

Jan explained that the Arapaho expected Tildie to bear the bulk of their burden. Women and dogs traditionally carried all as the semi-nomadic tribe moved around. He chortled. "The women particularly like when I tell how Jesus often honored women and sought to make their burdens less onerous. They are in favor of following our God in this area."

Jan provided each of his fellow travelers with a walking stick. The girls had animal heads carved at the top knob. Little Evie soon found herself carried by the big Swede in a sling much like the Indians used to carry their smallest children.

They marched toward the mountains for several hours, then Jan called a halt under a shade tree next to a brook. They ate the bread Older One had given them and settled in for a nap. While the hot September sun beat down on the dry land and the winds flowed down off the mountainside, they would rest.

In the tepee of Older One, Jan slept with the little family group. He had nestled between Mari and Boister. Next to Mari had been Evie with Tildie near the outside wall. Now, as they prepared to sleep in the shade of the elm, Mari plopped down beside Jan. Evie and Tildie took up the other blanket.

Tildie watched Boister stand undecided. Obviously, he didn't want to lie on a blanket with the girls nor settle beside Jan Borjesson. Finally, he sat between the two blankets with his back against the tree trunk.

When Tildie awoke hours later, he was a crumpled figure,

alone at the base of the tree. Her heart stirred with helplessness. Nothing she did seemed to bring Boister back to his childhood. He never fully interacted with anyone. She had thought that in the Indian village, he was showing some signs of attachment to the men and boys who included him in their daily lives.

He must feel sad over parting from his Indian friends. He had found something there with the other boys, despite their cultural differences. He'd been accepted. Even though he seldom spoke, or maybe, because he *was* such a little stoic, the Indian boys had included him in their games as well as their forages out into the countryside. Boister had brought with him a bow and set of arrows, a knife, and several other things Indian boys valued. Tildie didn't know exactly how he had acquired them. Perhaps the Indian men had given them to him as he learned alongside their sons.

Now Boister slept and he looked vulnerable like any other little six-year-old boy. The hard lines of his face were relaxed. He didn't look tough. Tildie knew he must grow up to be a man in this harsh world, but she regretted his loss of childish delight. She had never seen him giggle with abandon like the girls. She closed her eyes to pray and drifted from the comfort of the Father's presence into a peaceful sleep.

She awoke to the smell of dinner. Jan Borjesson grinned at her as she stretched and sat up. He crouched by a small fire, sitting on his heels and stirring the pot Boister had carried.

"Hmm, that's smells good."

"It's jerky and wild onions. Boister and I found a patch there by the stream. It still isn't cool enough to travel comfortably, so I figured we'd eat a bite first."

The breeze rustled the leaves above and played with the wisps of curly blond hair that framed Tildie's face. Her cheeks and the tip of her nose were red from the sun. Tildie reached up and pulled out the braid that hung down her back. With her fingers, she combed through the tangles and proceeded to redo the braid in a more orderly fashion.

The girls busily constructed a house out of sticks and leaves. Boister sat on a rock by the stream.

"There's a trading post two days west," said Jan, watching her as he stirred. "I have some credit there. We'll get a horse and some supplies. Think you can fashion a bonnet out of whatever material old Jake has available?"

"I'll certainly try." She looked down at her deerskin dress. "I don't look like an Indian or a white woman. Much longer in the sun and I'll be red and blistering."

"I was just thinking how nice it was to have company," Jan said with an admiring glance. His next words ruined any illusion Tildie had of her attractive appearance. "I guess I'm not too particular on what my company looks like, whether you're burnt or not. I've lived out here now for six years, and in that time, I've seen two white women. One was old Jake's wife. She died four winters ago. The other was a French woman traveling with a trapper. She didn't speak any English, Swedish, or Indian. Her trapper friend didn't want her talking to anyone, anyway. Jealous-type."

Tildie smiled, thinking how the trapper had cause to be jealous. Jan Borjesson was a man who would turn any woman's head.

"So you're Swedish. I thought so. We had a Swedish community in Lafayette."

"My grandparents came from Sweden and lived in Ohio. My parents live in the same farmhouse my grandpa built. I'm the oldest of thirteen children."

"The Indian women only have three or four children each. I thought that odd."

"Not when you consider that a man might have three wives. Then he is supporting nine to twelve children."

Tildie's eyes grew big. "I hadn't noticed that." She thought for a moment. "The Indian who wanted me, did he have other wives?"

Jan laughed. "You would've been wife number four. The

elders weren't too happy with his greed."

Tildie blushed. Jan continued, ignoring her discomfort. "He also had a passel of kids. He must have admired you quite a bit to be willing to take on three more."

He laughed again, but the thought sobered Tildie. She looked over to where the children sat happily engaged in their own activities.

"That's going to be a problem." She sighed. "They're good children, but I can't imagine how I'm going to provide for them. The homestead was profitable when Uncle Henry was alive, but John Masters pretty much ruined it. I'll have to depend on the foreman to turn it back into a working ranch."

"There's a foreman taking care of things?"

"Yes, George Taylor. He's probably getting more done without John Masters underfoot."

"Tell me about the ranch."

Tildie began with what she knew from the letters they had received from her aunt and uncle after the two headed west to settle. Boister came over to sit beside her, soaking up the information about his parents' early life.

"Uncle Henry had a way about him," said Tildie. "He was a friend to everyone. He was strong and ready to lend a helping hand to anyone. There were just a handful of settlers in their group, and he became their leader.

"He was helping with a load of rock. They were gathering the stones from a streambed to make a chimney in a neighbor's house. The load tipped, and he and the wagon went down the bank in a landslide."

Boister took hold of her hand. "I got to him first," he said. "Everyone was yelling, 'stay back,' but I didn't mind 'em. Pa was dead."

Tildie gave him a squeeze with the arm she draped across his back. His scrawny frame tensed as he leaned against her. It was the first time she'd ever heard him say anything about the accident. She knew it was a monumental step for the little boy but wasn't sure how to respond. He probably didn't want her to make a fuss, so she plunged on with the story.

"Aunt Matilda had never been without someone to guide her. First it was her father, my grandpa. Then when he died, it was her brother. She married Uncle Henry when she was eighteen. They lived in Lafayette for two years before he decided to move west.

"After he died, she needed someone to help her. Unfortunately, John Masters came along and sweet-talked her into believing he was the answer to her prayers. He wanted the house Uncle Henry had already built, fields that were already plowed and sown, and the thriving cattle spread Henry already started.

"Once they were married, John showed his true colors and browbeat my aunt and the children. He got drunk regularly and drove off most of the hands.

"When I came, there was no help in the house anymore. Aunt Matilda had Evelyn, who was almost a year old. Aunt Matilda had given up, just quit."

Tildie stared off into the distance remembering the woman who came to the door when she knocked. Thin, aged, with vacant eyes, she stood there, not recognizing her favorite niece. Her face and demeanor were so altered, Tildie thought she had come to the wrong house. With dawning horror, she realized this pathetic woman was the aunt who had played with her when she was young. This was the vibrant young woman whose earlier kindness had won a place in Tildie's heart forever.

She had reached out and took the thin, rough hands of her aunt. "Aunt Matilda, it's Tildie. . . ."

The guide she'd hired to bring her from the nearest settlement realized something was wrong. "Miss, this is the right place. Weren't you expected?"

"I wrote a letter. . ."

The door opened wider and John Masters pushed Matilda

aside to stand in the doorway. His feet apart, his arms crossed over his chest, he looked at the uninvited guest with barefaced contempt. "We wrote back, 'don't come,' " he growled. "I got enough mouths to feed. I took on two brats when I married your aunt, and we have a gal of our own. You're not needed here. If you could ride a horse and work the cattle, that'd be different. Can't keep decent help out here." He turned, pushing Matilda out of the way again, and stomped back into the dark house.

"You want me to take you back to the way station? A stage will be coming through next week. Take you back East," offered the guide.

"No."

The word was but a whisper. It didn't come from his passenger, but from the woman in the door. Aunt Matilda took hold of Tildie's arm and looked her full in the face. Her eyes filled with tears and the grip on Tildie's arm tightened. "Stay. Please stay."

"Yes, Aunt Matilda, I'll stay."

seven

Jan handed Tildie a bowl of soup. She took it absent-mindedly. Evie toddled over to thump herself down on the ground next to her cousin. The tousle-headed charmer held her chubby hands out to Jan with a irresistible smile and said, "Please."

"You want some soup, too?"

Jan dipped out the broth and handed it to the little girl. "Be careful. It's hot!" he warned.

"Hot. Blow," she commanded and held the bowl in front of Tildie's face. Tildie turned from her memories to involve herself in helping Evie cool her soup. Evie handled her spoon very well, even though she hadn't seen her second birthday yet.

"Hot. Blow," she said repeatedly, making them laugh as she dipped the spoon into the crude bowl, then held it out for different people to blow. Some soup was spilled, but not enough to cry over.

Tildie admired Jan's way with Evie. Some men didn't know how to handle a toddler's enthusiasm. Jan took it as a matter of course that Evie's soup needed to be blown, and some spoonfuls required a blow from each and every one of her dinner partners. He had as much fun joining in her foolishness as the family.

Eventually, they had to resume their long trek. They watched the sun set over the Rockies as they followed it west. Jan informed them that the mountains originally had been called, 'Shining Mountains,' and Tildie agreed it was more than appropriate.

Evie soon rode in the sling again, hanging on Jan's side. When Mari got tired, they stopped to shift the loads. Tildie got Evie and the sling. Jan hoisted Mari onto his back. He shortened his long stride so Boister and Tildie had to do less scurrying to keep up with him.

As they walked, he told stories. Some were of his travels in the wild, unsettled plains. Others were of his childhood. His Swedish grandmother had a store of Old World folktales, and Jan related them with a heavy Swedish accent. The accent alone sent the children into peals of laughter. The travel seemed easy with the merry sound of laughter and eager questions.

Tildie was distracted. She barely listened and didn't join in. Her mind dwelt on the time she spent living with her aunt and John Masters. Again, she felt the cold fury toward the man who had come into her aunt's life and made a bad situation so much worse. She stewed on his meanness and missed the humor in the stories Jan told.

Silver clouds scuttered across the moon. The night breeze gentled after the blustery day. They walked with only short rests until the travelers began to stumble over their own feet.

In spite of the long nap in the afternoon, the children settled down as soon as Jan and Tildie had the blankets rolled out. Tildie lay down as well, but she found it impossible to sleep. After a time, she gave up and went to sit on the trunk of a fallen tree, gazing out over the moon drenched landscape. Gladys plopped at her feet, quickly going back to sleep with her chin on Tildie's bare toes. When the dog raised her head sharply and gave a muffled woof of greeting, Tildie looked over her shoulder to see the huge form of the Swede coming towards her.

"Can't sleep?" He sat beside her.

"I'm sorry if I woke you."

"I'm used to Gladys being tucked up beside me. When she moved, I wondered why."

"It's beautiful, isn't it?" She waved a hand gesturing to the slightly rolling hills and the towering mountains beyond.

"It is." They sat in silence for a while.

Out of the stillness of the night came an owl's call, "Who cooks for you? Who cooks for you all?"

"What was that?" asked Tildie, brought out of her reflective mood by the strange, mellow sound.

"It's a barred owl. It could be almost a mile away."

"Who cooks for you? Who cooks for you all?" the owl repeated.

"It's eerie," observed Tildie. "Are you sure it's far away? It sounds so near."

"No, I'm not sure. The sound carries so well, he could be in one of the trees above us or clear across the field."

"It sounds like he asked who's cooking."

Jan chuckled. "He has another cry." Just as he finished his sentence, a shrill, cat-like scream rent the air. Tildie jumped and grabbed Jan's arm.

"That's it," laughed Jan.

"Did he kill something? Wasn't that the cry of his victim?"

"No, that was his other call. I always thought he was venting his frustration because no one answers when he asks who's cooking."

"Who cooks for you? Who cooks for you all?" came the call on the still night air.

Tildie laughed. "We should answer him. I don't want him getting frustrated again."

They were silent for awhile, listening to the night sounds. A slight breeze whispered through the leaves above. The brook bubbled over the round stones. A plop in the water sounded nearby, and Tildie lifted an inquiring eyebrow at Jan.

"Toad, most probably."

She nodded, confident that Jan would be able to identify any of the mysterious night sounds.

Jan watched her as though puzzled. "Why are you disturbed? You've been quiet since you told me about John Masters's and your aunt's spread. The children joined in the talk as we walked, but you seemed far away."

Tildie turned her face from his scrutiny. He was a missionary, a man of God. Would he understand the torment she'd felt since the day John Masters died?

"You tell people about Christ, don't you?" Her words were a bare whisper hovering among the quiet sounds of the night. "You tell them how to be saved?"

"Yes."

"How do you feel when someone believes in Jesus, accepts Him?"

"I feel good." Jan shrugged, baffled by her question.

"Have you ever hated the one who accepted Christ? Have you ever wanted to take the words back, wished you hadn't spoken, wanted the man in hell?" Tildie voice remained low, vibrating with the pent-up rage she'd been hiding.

"Who, Tildie?"

"John Masters." She drew her knees up until her feet rested on the wide log and her arms wrapped tightly around her legs. She bowed her head against her knees, hiding her face. "I hate him. I can't let go of the feelings. While he was alive, we just tried to get through each day without having more trouble than we needed. I didn't realize how much I hated him.

"He destroyed what my uncle had built. He destroyed my aunt. Boister has never recovered from his father's death, and that can be laid at John Masters's door, too. The girls were mistreated. He even hit them when he was drunk. Once he swung at me. I ducked and he fell into the fireplace. He hit his head and was out cold. I pulled him out, and Aunt Matilda and I wrapped his burned hand with salve and clean linen strips. We left him to sleep it off on the hearth rug.

"I didn't feel the anger then, but when he was lying there, dying in the Indian tepee, rage surged inside of me."

She turned her face to rest her cheek on her knees, and Jan saw wet streaks. Until that moment, he hadn't realized she was crying. Her cold, dispassionate voice hid the tears.

He laid a hand on her back, and she closed her eyes, relaxing somewhat in the comfort of his touch. Taking a deep breath, she let it out slowly. It came in a shudder, and her lovely features tightened into a grimace as she tried to control her feelings. Jan's hand stroked up and down her back in a soothing motion.

"Tell me about it, Tildie."

She couldn't face him as she spoke, so Tildie lifted her head to stare off and away from the lonely spot where they sat. "I don't know what I was thinking I would say when I managed to sneak away from Older One and crossed the village. I knew he was dying. I had to see him, but really didn't know why.

"He was mangled, and the smell was horrid. He looked so dirty and disgusting. All the times he was drunk, I never felt pity for him, and all of a sudden, I was sorry for him." She paused, remembering the confusion of strong feelings.

"I hated him. Aunt Matilda was already dead. He was supposed to take care of her. He didn't, and she was dead. He was supposed to take care of the children, and he was going to die and leave them and me alone in that Indian village. Any minute he would slip away. I starting telling him how horrid he was, how mean and low-down. He was dying, and I was railing at him."

She paused again, almost too ashamed to go on. Jan waited.

"He heard me. He said I shouldn't talk to a dying man like that, and then I was telling him to repent because he was going to hell. I didn't hear him say the words, but I know he did. I could see it on his face when he was dead. That despicable, low-down worm of a man had a look of complete and utter peace on his face, and I was angrier than ever. He'd made so many people suffer, and he didn't get punished. I didn't want him to get off scot-free."

The last words came out in sobs and Jan put his arm around her. First she stiffened and drew away, but the emotion had too hard a grip on her. She leaned against him, trying to stifle the sobs against his chest.

She thought of the sleeping children and didn't want them to waken. As in the lonely nights in the Indian encampment, she desperately did not want them to see her weak. She must be strong for them. . .and how could she explain the bitter tears of hatred for their stepfather? How could she be an example of a strong and loving Christian when she was so weak and full of hatred?

"There, there, Tildie. Cry it all out." Jan spoke softly into her hair, rocking her gently in his arms. After a bit, the violent, wracking sobs subsided. She rested within the curve of his arm.

"You know, he did suffer," Jan said.

"He was in terrible pain from his injuries," agreed Tildie. The shame of her verbal attack on a dying man softened her voice.

"Yes, but I was meaning every day of his life."

Tildie pulled back from him and took out the scrap of calico she still used as a handkerchief. She blew her nose and wiped her tears.

"What do you mean?" she asked.

"If you know a person who acts like he did, you can walk away from him. Some of them, you can walk away and never deal with again. Some of them, you can at least have a moment's peace from time to time away from their distemper. But imagine *being* that person. You could never get away for even a moment. Even in your dreams, you would still be the despicable character everyone hates."

She leaned against him again, and he held her close to his side.

"I never thought of that." Tildie sighed.

"There must have been a lot of hate in that man, and as much as he aimed his hatred at you and his family, he aimed more at himself. He knew he wasn't as good a man as your

Uncle Henry. That probably made him meaner. Even in his evil intent to take over the ranch and live a life of ease, he failed. Do you think he ever succeeded at anything?"

"Probably not," she admitted.

"Do you think he liked himself for taking a good thing and making it bad?"

"He said it was the lazy hands, bad weather, and coyotes. He had an excuse for every failure."

"And did you believe the excuses?"

"No," she said strongly.

"Do you think he really believed them?"

"No," she said quietly.

"He was a miserable man, and he suffered every day of his life just because he was stuck being himself. He knew of no way to change. He didn't have our Savior to ease his pain and lead him to a better way."

"I haven't been a good Christian, Jan. In the Indian camp, I asked God to help me and didn't expect Him to listen. God knows He had to force me to talk to John about salvation. I didn't want to, and God knows how angry I am that John didn't go to hell." She hiccuped on another sob. "Jan, that sounds so horrible. Everytime the thought goes through my head, I'm ashamed. How can God even stand for me to call on His Name?"

"Well, let's count your sins. One, you hated a hateful man. Two, you begrudgingly helped him to Heaven. Three, you're angry with God for forgiving him. Four, you doubt God is good enough to forgive you of your sins. Five, you doubt God is strong enough to help you conquer the resentment and hatred and provide for you and the kids all at the same time. Maybe, the last one should count as three. One for resentment, one for hatred, and one for thinking He wouldn't take care of you. That makes seven."

Tildie leaned back to look at his face, uncertain as to where his list would lead her.

"How many times did Christ say we were to forgive?" he asked.

"Seventy times seven."

"Uh-huh. Maybe because he figured that was about all we were capable of. Personally, I think He just meant not to be keeping score." Jan shifted and gave her shoulders a squeeze. "Now God, being God, should be able to forgive a whole lot more sins than a human's puny four hundred and ninety. Doesn't that figure?"

"Yes."

"And, since He doesn't keep count, having lost previous sins in the depths of the ocean, it figures He could handle your seven sins."

Tildie nodded.

"Now, taking under consideration that you're going to repent of these seven sins, what we have left is how you're going to deal with them in the future."

She nodded again.

"Number One, hating the hateful man. Best just say you're sorry for taking over God's job of being judge and jury. Then, forget about that one. Number Two, telling the Gospel through clenched teeth, so to speak. Thank Him for using you anyway and move on to number three. What was Number Three?"

Tildie thought for a moment.

"Being angry with God for forgiving John."

Jan nodded and was silent for a moment. "Best just say you're working on getting over it and ask for some help. Number Four, doubting God is ready and willing to forgive you of your sins. Thank Him for waiting for you like the father waited for the prodigal son and tell Him you're ready for any fatted calves with your name on them. Might say you're sorry again. It'll make you feel better.

"Number Five, Six, and Seven—anger, resentment, and lack of trust. Phew! Guess you're just a lowly, no-good follower like Peter, Paul, doubting Thomas, Barnabas, and Mark to name a few."

Tildie gasped. She looked at his earnest face and saw kindness there. Shyly, a smile warmed her face. He was right. She had been trying so hard to overcome her weaknesses, she'd been so busy browbeating herself for her failures, she'd forgotten how great God is.

"Thank you, Jan." She hugged him. "Sometimes when you talk to me, I feel like my own father is giving me advice."

"Your father?" Jan's eyebrows rose an inch.

"Yes, he was a schoolteacher and a strong Christian. He always seemed to have words of wisdom from the Bible. He was so mature and stable. With him around, I felt secure."

"You feel secure with me?"

"Yes, I trust you. More than I would have trusted my own big brother, Daniel. Daniel was good with figures. He worked in a bank, but he wouldn't have known how to handle this, and he certainly wouldn't have walked across the plains of Colorado."

Jan sat quietly for a moment. "So, what happened to your big brother?"

"Influenza. My parents, too. It took almost one third of the population of Lafayette in seven weeks."

His arms tightened around her. There was so much sadness in her past. He wanted to protect her, make the days ahead comfortable and easy for her. Maybe he was feeling protective like a father. Her warm compact body fit so snugly against his side. No, he definitely was not feeling fatherly. He let her go and slapped his hands on his knees. "Well, since I remind you of your father and older brother, I best act like one of 'em and shoo you to bed. We have a long walk ahead of us tomorrow."

She stood up and looked down at him. "Thank you again, Jan. I feel much better."

"Sure," he said as she turned and walked back to the blankets where the little ones slept.

Jan stooped to ruffle the fur around Gladys's neck and spoke so only his canine companion could hear. "Seems like I'm not much interested in being like a father or an older brother to Miss Matilda Harris."

He sighed and looked out into the vast starry sky.

"Father in Heaven," he prayed. "What are You proposing I do about this?" Taking advice he'd handed out to others, Jan decided to pray and sleep on it.

eight

Tildie stood on the hill overlooking a man-made structure that barely marred the landscape. They'd reached the trading post. Disappointment dragged at her steps as she followed the skipping children down the gentle slope. They were excited to reach anyplace. Jan said this hovel held a wonderment of goods. Tildie swallowed hard against the tears. She chided herself. Had she expected Brenner's Mercantile on Main Street Lafayette?

The building proved to be little more than a man's sod house with shelves lining the only room. She found no material she could use to make a skirt, blouse, bonnet, or anything that would get her out of the Indian garb. This didn't bother her as much as it would have three months earlier. She liked the feel of the heavy leather. It was actually cooler than cotton, which would have clung to her as she perspired. As they walked through the brush, her Indian dress and leggings didn't catch in the branches as a white woman's clothing would.

With no bonnets available, Jan bought her a comb and a man's hat from the three men's hats on the shelf. Her image in the warped shiny tin piece Jake used as a mirror made her grin. She looked a vision with her pale deerskin dress, two long blond braids hanging down, topped with a black felt hat. Jan also bought a hat for Boister. Boister's face was a nut brown. Tildie's was beet red, having burned, peeled, and burned again. Jake recommended some ointment for her burnt skin.

Jan bought three horses. Since he'd made no purchases just for the little girls, he told them they could name the horses.

Mari named hers Charger, remembering a story Tildie had told her about knights in England who rode noble steeds. An undistinguished roan with a sway back, but good teeth, Charger hardly looked the part his name implied. Soon they fell to calling him Charlie.

Evie insisted her horse be called "Horse."

When Jan turned to Boister with a question in his eye, Boister walked over to the third horse, a bay, and stroked her shoulder and neck as high as he could reach.

"Do you want to name her?" asked Jan.

The horse bent her head and nuzzled Boister around the neck and down the front of his shirt, looking for a treat.

"Greedy Gert." Boister smiled. He reached in his pocket and pulled out a dried apple slice he'd gotten from Jake. Greedy Gert lipped it out of his palms and scarfed it down quickly.

Two old saddles came with the horses. The harnesses looked decrepit, but Jan thought them usable. Boister rode Greedy Gert with only an Indian girth. Tildie held Evie in front of her on Horse, and Jan carried Mari on Charlie. They made good time on the trail, bypassed Fort Reynald, and headed up a canyon beyond Manitou Springs in just a couple of days.

"We've got to get up into that tree line." Jan came back from leading their little procession to ride beside her.

Tildie looked up the steep embankment to the thick fir trees. It would be a hard climb and once there; the going would be rough.

"Why? The way is easier here," she protested.

"Air's cooled off considerable in the last few minutes. Look at the sky—clouds are gathering from the west. It's raining in the mountains. The reason there's no tall growth in this canyon is it's a run-off. Down here we could be caught in a flash flood. We're going up to be safe."

Tildie nodded her head, thanking God Jan knew these things. She never would have picked up the signs. She'd been daydreaming about the ranch, wondering what life would be like in the little house with just her and the children—and without Jan. She was getting used to having him around.

Jan dismounted and led Mari on the horse up the side of the incline. Boister followed with Evie and Tildie bringing up the rear.

They progressed slowly. The wind picked up as they neared the crest, and Tildie became aware of a steady roar distinctly different from the bluster of the wind.

"Jan, I hear something."

"I hear it, too. Concentrate on where you're going."

Gladys stood at the top watching their climb. She added her encouragement in urgent, sharp barks.

A few heavy raindrops pelted them in huge drops. The cadence of their sharp ping against the rocks picked up. Soon the torrent forced Tildie to duck her head and bend over Evie to protect the child with her body. Horse blew through her nostrils expressing her displeasure and Charlie answered. Horse tossed her head and tried to push past the middle horse.

Jan quickened the pace. The noise grew louder and, although Tildie had never had experience with the sound, she knew it was deadly and coming down the canyon. She could no longer hear Gladys's bark. She couldn't hear the horses or Jan—nothing but the deafening roar of rampaging water and great rumblings of thunder.

Jan and Mari climbed over the edge. He tied the reins around a branch and lifted Mari down, then turned to hasten Boister's mount. "Dismount and tie him off, Boister," he shouted over the roar.

The rain dissolved the ground into a slippery mass. A crack of thunder broke above them, and Horse reared, lost her footing, then fell sideways against the rocks. Tildie let go of the reins and, with both arms around Evie, tried to clear the falling horse. She flew backwards and to the side, fortunately next to the mountain, not the drop to the crevasse below. She twisted so Evie was on top of her, trying not to let go or fall on her. Tildie heard the horse scream in terror and sensed Horse's hooves scrabbling for purchase right beside her. A hoof caught her on the side, and as she rolled, her head struck something. A flash of light, immediately followed by a crash of thunder, echoed the pain within her skull. Evelyn screeched.

Through a haze of pain, Tildie saw Jan above her. He wrenched Evie from her hold and turned to pass the little girl to her brother right behind him. Jan pulled Tildie to her feet. She gasped as pain enveloped her right side. The Swede took no notice and half dragged her up the last few feet to safety. She could hear nothing but the roar. A great wall of muddy water, carrying logs, small boulders, and other debris passed beneath them. With the swirling waters just inches from their feet, Jan pulled her higher over the ridge.

The noise level dropped immediately. Tildie heard Evie and Mari crying. She turned from Jan's arms to reach them. A pain pierced her back high between the shoulder blades, and blackness engulfed her.

Vaguely, she became aware of sounds and movement beside her. Rain splashed on her face, but she couldn't lift her hands to wipe it away. The rain and wind still pounded the earth, but the thunder muttered in the distance. A small, cold rivulet of rain ran through the mud by her side. Tildie could feel it, knew it was there, but couldn't move away. She tried to open her eyes, to speak, but the effort was too much. She slipped again into oblivion.

She was cold. She could hear a fire crackling, but she couldn't move toward it. She tried to open her eyes. She couldn't. There was something warm on each side of her. The girls. She was between the girls. It was so cold. She gave up trying. It was better to sleep.

"Tildie, drink this," a voice commanded her. Someone lifted her head and shoulders. It hurt. *Please*, she begged. *Leave me alone*. No words came. The warm broth dribbled down her throat and down her chin. She tried to swallow. *Leave me alone*, she wanted to cry. She swallowed.

The voices. Sometimes she recognized the voices. Evie chanting her version of a lullaby. Mari asking for something. A cup? Her supper? Tildie couldn't quite hear.

Quiet. The world smelled wet. Smoke drifted from a fire, filled with the acrid odor of soggy wood trying to burn. The wool of the wet blanket stank. She wanted to move.

Someone moved her gently, but it felt like she was being tossed from side to side. *Don't*, she screamed but knew there was no sound. *Please, please, please let me be.*

Warmer. The sun beat down on her. Now the blanket smelled musty. Mari repeated a counting rhyme in a sing-song voice.

"Pick it up. Lay it out. One for baby. Don't you pout. Pick it up. Lay it out. Two for brother, inside out. Pick it up. Lay it out. One for sister. She can't count."

The sun was gone. A voice mumbled in her ear. On one side the warmth of a small figure curled against her side. On the other, a body stretched full-length beside her. A warm arm rested over her stomach. A heavy thigh nestled against her own. She could feel his breath on her cheek. She heard the words.

"Heavenly Father, bring her through this. Heal her, Lord. I've done all I can. Give her strength. Give her life. Give her healing. Bless her. I thank you for bringing her into my life. I thank you for Marilyn, Evelyn, and Boister. They need her, Lord. Heal her. Make her recover." The words went on, and Tildie slept.

She opened her eyes. Over her was an impromptu lean-to fashioned out of cut and woven branches. She moved her head to the side. A neat, small fire blazed inside a circle of smooth round stones. Boister fed it sticks. Mari attempted to comb her own hair as she sat on a log, a little behind her brother. Beyond that, three horses were tied to a rope suspended between two trees.

So Horse had not plummeted to her death, nor bolted and run. With that thought came a conglomeration of memories, some distinct, others hazy and dreamlike. Tildie lay still, trying to sort them out.

The horses moved restlessly. One snorted, and one whinnied softly. Tildie heard Evie's chatter right before Jan strode into the little clearing with Evie riding his shoulders and Gladys trotting beside him. He tossed a dead rabbit to Boister, who caught it and held it up to admire. Jan reached up and, with one motion, grabbed a giggling Evie and swung her down to sit beside her sister. Tildie noted Evie's hair was cut in a rather rag-tag style, close to her head. With two long strides, Jan crossed the clearing and crouched beside her. His huge form blocked the sun and she couldn't see his face with the light behind him.

"You're awake." He waited for her to respond. When she didn't, he continued. "Are you thirsty? Do you want a drink?"

"Yes." The whisper was hardly audible.

"Mari, bring a cup of water," he called and sat down beside Tildie. He lifted her to a sitting position, her back against his chest. The pain seared through her, and even as it threatened to turn her stomach, she realized that the pain was not as intense as it had been during the long hours she'd slept and roused, barely conscious.

Mari brought the cup.

"Is she all right?" she asked.

Tildie had closed her eyes against the pain. She opened them to look into Mari's dear, little, concerned face. She tried to smile.

"Tildie, we thought you would die. We prayed," Mari whispered.

"I'm not going to die," she managed to say.

"Drink this." Jan had taken the cup. One of his strong arms supported her around the waist. The other hand held the cup to her lips. She drank, but even swallowing caused the pain to rise and ebb away. She paused.

"More," she whispered. The next sip brought less pain. She leaned her head back against Jan's shoulder and relaxed. It was then the blanket slipped, just enough to expose her bare shoulder. The cool air hit her skin, and she realized her dress was gone. She was wrapped in blankets. Her eyes grew wide, and she stared around the campsite. It had the look of a place that had been inhabited for awhile.

"How long?" she croaked.

"Eight days."

"My dress?"

"It was wet through, and you were cold."

"Evie's hair?"

"She cried when I combed it and it got more and more tangled. I cut it off." With the last admission, Jan's voice filled with regret.

" 'Sall right." The words came out slurred. "Grow."

"Is she all right?" asked Mari again. Boister seemed to just come aware of the activity in the lean-to. He'd been cleaning the rabbit. He came to the lean-to with bloody hands, holding a bloody knife.

"Is she awake? Will she live?" he asked.

Before Jan could answer, Tildie struggled to lean away from him.

"Sick," she muttered as she turned away from the gruesome sight of her cousin's hands. She fought the nausea and felt Jan's hand on her back.

"Go wash up, Boister. Yes, I think she's going to make it."

nine

Now she was used to sleeping in Jan's arms. For days, she had been getting stronger. The pain still hovered, but only as a ghost of its former self with sharp reminders when she breathed too deeply or suddenly moved.

At night, the children all nestled between her and the back of the lean-to. Jan lay down between her and the outside. He cradled her gently, and she relished the warmth that came through the blankets. He offered her no consideration for her modesty as she became better. He uninhibitedly helped her to slip the Indian dress over her head and gently lifted her while Marilyn pulled it down over her hips. He strapped the leggings back on her legs, and it was he who supported her when she was able to get up and go relieve herself in the woods. Several times, she fainted when the pain grabbed her after an ill-advised movement. He caught her and held her until she revived.

Once she woke up in the middle of the night, whimpering in his arms.

"Hush now, Honey," he crooned soothingly. "You're going to be all right. The pain will go away. You're going to live. You're going to get over this. Hush, now. I'm here." His voice calmed her as he spoke, some to her and some in entreaties to their Heavenly Father for mercy on her, healing, and strength.

Another week went by. She awoke one morning to frigid air and a dusting of powdery white snow on the ground.

Boister stirred the pot over the fire. The girls still huddled in their blankets at the back of the lean-to. Jan bent over a tree-pole construction.

"Jan," she called. He left his project immediately.

"Do you need to get up?" He knelt beside her.

"No, not yet. What are you doing?"

"I'm building a travois, an Indian litter for carrying you to my cabin. We can't stay here any longer."

"How far is it?"

"Not far as the crow flies, but we aren't crows." He smiled down at her, and she decided not to press him for answers.

She was better. She could almost put her weight on her legs, but she still couldn't take a step. She'd asked what he thought was wrong.

"I think a couple of broken ribs. You have a massive bruise on your back. There's even the outline of Horse's foot in deep purple. There may be some injury to your spine, though thank God, you don't seem to be paralyzed. Also, you had a concussion, and one leg was bruised from the knee up to your hip. I couldn't find sign of a broken bone, but it sure was one ugly bruise."

She was embarrassed that he had examined her so closely and turned the subject away from herself. "The children were all right?"

"Scared, cold, and worried, but no injuries. They've been real troopers, helping me to take care of you and not complaining." He paused. "They've been praying hard, too. We didn't know if you'd live."

"Jan, I'm so grateful."

He cut her off. "No, not a word. I'm just glad you're alive. Hey!" he lightened his tone. "After a week of being mother and father to three small kids, I'd have given you a good shake and told you to come back and help me out if you'd died."

"I'm sorry."

"No, don't be. Remember, I'm the oldest of thirteen. I know how to change diapers. By the way, Evie is now totally independent in that area."

"You trained her?" said Tildie, incredulous.

"Well, I took off the nappies completely and encouraged her to lift up her dress and squat. She's gotten very good at it."

Tildie started to laugh, but the pain caused her to groan instead—albeit with a smile on her lips.

When they started out, Evie and Mari rode double on the back of Horse with the travois attached behind. Jan lead the horse, and Gladys trotted beside Tildie's travois as if she had appointed herself guardian. Next, Boister held Charlie's reins. Greedy Gert followed docilely behind.

The travois consisted of two long poles attached to a harness over Horse's shoulders. The free ends dragged behind the horse with a blanket secured in a sling-like fashion between them. Tildie was strapped in and surrounded by most of their belongings.

It was two days' travel, and the days became a blur of jostling and pain for Tildie. She awoke the third night inside a cabin, lying on a pine needle bed with a heavy blanket beneath her and a quilt on top. She could hear the sound of the others' breathing and saw dimly a dying fire glowing in a fireplace across the room. Beyond that she could see the horses. She was confused. Was she in a cabin or a barn?

"Jan," she whispered into the dark.

There was a stirring beside the bed, and Jan's head appeared inches from hers.

"Are you all right? Do you need something?"

"We're at your cabin?"

"Yes."

"Where is everybody?

"Mari and Evie are over there on a pallet. Gladys and Boister are there." He pointed them out in the dim light. "Do you want a drink?"

"Yes."

He rose from his pallet in one fluid movement. She was astonished again at how well such a big man moved. He moved more like an Indian than a white man. Now that she had lived among the Arapaho, she could appreciate the difference. Very few white men had such grace.

He returned with the cup, handed it to her, and laughed softly when he had to rescue the cup before she dropped it. He helped her sit up, and she drank it all.

"Thank you."

He lowered her and put the cup on the floor. "Are you all right?" he asked again. "You feel feverish."

"I ache," she said but chose not to elaborate. "It feels strange to be sleeping by myself. After all, there have been six bodies in the lean-to for weeks."

"Six?"

"I was counting Gladys." She could feel herself getting sleepy again. "Are there horses in your living room?" she asked, not sure to trust her vision.

"Yes."

She looked at his strong face. He was smiling. "Jan, don't go away. I'm frightened tonight."

"Why?" He held her hand and smoothed the hair back from her hot, dry forehead.

"I think something's wrong. Inside. I don't think I'm going to live."

"Don't say that, Tildie."

She sighed, and the effort made her wince.

"You *are* going to live. You would've died by now if you were going to. Every day you're stronger."

"Not tonight, Jan. Something's wrong."

"Please, Tildie, don't talk like that. Rest."

"Jan, I'm glad you came to get us. I'm sorry I'm such a burden."

He leaned over and kissed her forehead. If possible, she was hotter than she had been only a few minutes before. "Tildie, don't do this. Don't die. You have to fight."

She was unconscious, and he stood abruptly, his hands

clenched at his sides. His chin came up, and he stared at the ceiling.

"Lord, I want this woman. Don't let her die. I feel like she's always been a part of my life. I loved her before I met her. She's the woman I knew I'd meet one day. God, you understand. She's my other part. She's kind and brave and laughs like a child when she's happy. Don't let her die. Tell me what to do for her. Don't take her away. Let me be her husband. Let me take care of her. Give her into my hands, Lord. Let me cherish her. God, don't take her."

The fever raged during the night. Jan brought snow in from outside and barely let it melt before dipping a rag into it and wiping her face, neck, and arms. When Boister awoke in the morning he helped. When Mari joined them a few minutes later, Jan took off the blanket that had been kicked about as she struggled against the fever. "Here, each of you take a rag and wash her legs with the cool water."

"Is she going to die now?" asked Mari.

"Is it because we moved her?" asked Boister.

"We had to leave," answered Jan. "Heavy snow fell last night. We got to the cabin just in time. God was with us in making that trip. He'll be with us through this."

The eyes of the two small children looked at him. They were scared, and he was, too. He knelt on the floor and gestured for them to come to him. They walked into his arms and held on to one another, taking comfort in the agony and hope that they shared.

"Pray, Mari. Pray, Boister." He had meant for them to pray throughout the day, but Mari took him literally. She folded her little hands in front of her. Still leaning heavily against him, she began, "God, we love Tildie. You already have Pa and Mama. We want Tildie to stay here. Please don't take her." Her little face screwed up, and she buried it in Jan's shoulder.

"God," said Boister. "I promise not to hate You for taking Pa and sending John Masters. I promise to listen to Jan's stories and learn to read the Bible. I won't hide when it's chore time. I won't tease Mari and Evie. I won't give Tildie a hard time when she wants me to practice my sums. I'll be good. Always. Please, don't let Tildie die."

Jan squeezed them, fighting the tears in his eyes. "You don't have to make a bargain with God, Boister. He wants to give us good things without making deals."

"I've been telling Him bad things in my head. I told Him He's no good 'cause He didn't do right by my family. I told Him He's mean and awful. He's going to take Tildie because I'm bad."

"No, Boister, no. That's not the way God works. People may act like that because people aren't holy like God, but God is bigger and better than people. God loves us, and He will take care of us. Even when we don't understand, He is faithful. He is just. He's in control. We must trust Him. We have to, Boister. He wants to bless us. I don't understand why all this has happened. I do know that I love your cousin. If you hadn't been in that Indian camp, I never would have met her."

"If He kills her now, it don't mean much," sobbed Boister.

"God doesn't kill people." Jan sounded desperate now. How could he explain so the little boy would understand? What was Mari thinking? Was she just as confused? "Sometimes He takes people to Heaven because it would be too hard on them down here. Think of all the pain Tildie's been in. What if that were to go on forever? In Heaven, she won't hurt any more. She'll be well."

"Do you want her to die?" Boister's voice was small and choked.

"No, I want her to live. But that's what I want. That isn't necessarily what God wants. Maybe that isn't what's best for Tildie. We have to give up what we want and ask God to do what's best for her. It's not your fault she's sick."

"I pushed the wagon." His voice was so low, Jan almost

couldn't make out the words.

"What?"

"The wagon with the rocks. One wheel was stuck. I pushed it to get it over the rock, and I stumbled and hit it sideways. It slid over the edge. It killed my Pa."

"How old were you, Boister?"

"Three."

"And you remember this?"

Boister nodded his downcast head. "I dream about it. I think about it every day. I can hear the men shouting. I hear the rocks and the wagon creaking."

"Boister, you were three. Look at Mari, how little she is. You were a little boy. That wagon must have weighed a ton. Boister, you couldn't have knocked it off the path with your puny little shove. It was going anyway. You didn't do it. You were too little."

"I did it. I fell and it slid away, down the bank. I did it."

There was desperation in his voice and Jan knew it was important to get through to him. "Boister, no. You didn't do it." Jan sent up a quick plea for help. What could he say to relieve this child's anguish? "Boister, remember the rock at the camp—the one you climbed on? You couldn't move that rock, could you?"

Boister shook his head.

"*I* couldn't even move that rock, Boister. Even if we got it in a wagon, I couldn't move the wagon. If you took all the smaller rocks that your Pa and those men had been moving that day, and put them together, they would have been about as big as that rock. Boister, you didn't knock the wagon over. You couldn't have. It's just a coincidence that you bumped it just as it was going over anyway." Jan, with one arm still securely around Mari, tilted his head to look at Boister's partially hidden face. "Do you understand, Boister? You could *not* have moved that wagon."

Boister's shoulders shook, and Jan held him closer. Soon,

the sobs broke out, and the little boy shuddered as all the pent-up guilt released.

Evie woke and Mari slipped over to talk quietly to her as Jan rocked Boister in his arms.

Later as they ate breakfast, Boister stirred his mash with little enthusiasm. Jan watched him but said nothing. To his eye, the boy looked more relaxed. Jan could only pray the talk had done him good.

For a day-and-a-half more, Tildie was delirious, fighting the fever and sometimes lashing out at Jan as he put the cooling cloths on her forehead. During the second night, the fever broke. The children awoke to find both Jan and Tildie sleeping soundly. Boister told the girls to be quiet, and he sliced them biscuits from two days before and gave them warmed water to drink.

The girls quietly played with their two dolls while Boister attempted to clean up. They needed more firewood, so he bundled up, admonished the girls to be quiet, and took Gladys out to gather what he could find.

ten

"We're cold." Mari tugged at Jan's sleeve.

"Code," agreed Evie, bobbing her head up and down.

Jan stretched and looked over at Tildie. She was sleeping restfully on the pine needle mattress. He reached for his boots and pulled them on. The room was chilly, the fire almost out.

"I'll go out and get some firewood."

"Boister already did."

Jan looked quickly about the cabin. Boister was nowhere in sight. He sprang to his feet and grabbed his heavy blanket coat.

"How long has he been gone?"

"Since we ate breakfast."

Gladys was gone, too. Maybe nothing was wrong. Gladys could lead him back to the cabin. Jan wrapped a scarf around his neck and pulled a knitted cap down over his ears. He opened the door to the blaring light of sun on mountain snow.

He hurried around the corner, kicked the snow off a couple of smaller logs and brought them in. Repeating the process several times, he soon had the fire blazing.

"Mari, I have to leave you in charge of Evie and Tildie. Keep Evie away from the fire. If Tildie wakes up, give her some water and a biscuit to chew on." The little girl nodded solemnly. Jan kissed her good-bye on the forehead and ruffled her hair. He gave Evie a quick peck and looked one last time at Tildie.

"I'll be back as soon as I can." He opened the door and plunged into the deep snow, following the tracks left by Boister and Gladys.

No new snowfall obscured their tracks into the woods.

With Jan's long stride reaching over the heavy snow, he quickly covered the territory Boister had plowed through in his meandering.

When Jan found Boister, he had the strong urge to yank him up by the back of his pants and blister him good. All manner of disasters had plagued his thoughts as possible explanations for the boy not returning.

Boister and Gladys lay in the snow, scrutinizing the most makeshift rabbit trap Jan had ever seen. Built with the Indian snare in mind, it had some imaginative white boy innovations which would not have held a weak, blind rabbit for the time it took it to turn around, but boy and dog were entranced with the contraption.

Jan did nothing to cover the sound of his approach and Boister and Gladys turned eagerly to greet him, jumping up to run to him.

"Look, Jan," Boister pointed to his trap. "If we wait awhile, we'll have rabbit stew for dinner. I thought some rabbit meat would make Tildie feel better. You know, give her the broth."

"That's a good idea, son, but I need you back at the cabin. We'll hunt up some meat for dinner for sure. Come on, now. Tildie's better, and if she wakes to find us gone, she'll be worried."

Boister abandoned his trap immediately. "I was gathering twigs for kindling and then I got to thinking how they would bend and make a trap. It's not exactly how White Feather taught me, but. . ." He looked over his shoulder at the trap. "Can we check it tomorrow? Or, should we take it apart? I don't want a rabbit to get stuck in it and die if we aren't going to eat it."

Jan didn't have the heart to tell him the first stiff wind would collapse the contraption, so he shrugged. "We'll check it tomorrow."

They went back to the house to find Tildie still asleep and the girls playing their neverending game of putting dolls to bed, waking them up to feed them, and putting them back to bed.

In the evening, Tildie awoke. She sipped on venison broth, courtesy of Jan's afternoon hunt. The next day, she sat up on her bed. A few days later, she sat in a chair.

"Jan, these children *smell*," she said, wrinkling her nose over Evie's shorn head.

Jan looked up from the snare he was helping Boister craft. His head shook slightly from side to side in bewilderment.

"Didn't your mother make all twelve of your sisters and brothers take a bath from time to time?" Tildie's eyebrows arched over her eyes.

"Yes, but we had a tub and towels and something beside old lye soap."

"Jan, you and I stink as well."

"What do you propose we do about it?"

"We'll give the children a standing bath."

"A standing bath?"

"We need two pails."

Jan looked over at the area beside the fireplace where he put together his food. He wouldn't exactly call it a kitchen, but it had a pretty good sized kettle. His mind wandered over his meager possessions.

"There's a bucket I use to feed the horses."

Tildie looked towards the stable end of the cabin. In an economy of heating, it attached to the house with only a half wall between the main room and the stalls. The children thought this was marvelous and visited with the horses regularly.

Jan explained that the heat of the horses' bodies helped warm the cabin, and in the dead of winter, he didn't have to worry about them being in a drafty stable freezing to death. Of course, the stable room had originally been built for a horse and a pack mule, but the three new tenants were comfortable, if crowded.

"What became of the original tenants?" Tildie had asked.

"Traded them."

"For what?"

"Books."

"Books?"

He shrugged. "Winter before last, I read to the animals every book I owned two or three times each. Gladys and I don't mind walking. We didn't really need the horse and mule once we were settled in.

"Gladys is good company during the winter months, but the books truly were better companions than the horses, and I didn't have to feed them every day and clean out their stalls."

Boister laughed. He threw back his head and laughed. The girls looked up in surprise, and they laughed too, more to be joining in the merriment than realizing what had struck their big brother as funny. Tildie who had never seen her cousin laugh, smiled with tears in her eyes. Gladys began to bounce around him and added her bark to the hullabaloo. Jan swept down on the boy and tickled him until Boister begged him to stop. Mari and Evie joined in by tackling Jan and claiming they could save their brother.

Eventually the fun subsided, and the four lay in mock exhaustion on the floor.

"I haven't forgotten the baths," said Tildie.

"Our babies need a bath, too." Mari reached out to rescue her doll, which had been carelessly thrown aside.

Evie bobbed her head in agreement and crawled over to where her doll lay upside down against the wall.

"So does Gladys, Tildie," pointed out Boister.

Jan drew the line at the dog. "Only humans are getting bathed this winter," he declared.

Mari's lower lip came out in a pout. "Sarah is 'uman." She squeezed her beloved playmate.

Jan looked to Tildie for advice.

"The dollies can take a bath with you. Just hold on to them, and they'll get plenty clean." She hoped this would suffice. It was going to be a chore just washing bodies and clothes.

They heated the water in the kettle, then they stripped down Evie first, standing her in the horses' feed bucket. With Tildie's supervision from her chair, Mari and Jan wet down the giggling girl, soaped her up, and sponged her off. She was wrapped in a large piece of blanket and relegated to Tildie's lap while the process was repeated for Marilyn.

As long as Evie did not wiggle too much, Tildie enjoyed having her in her lap. The little girl settled quietly, with only a reminder that too much bouncing hurt her cousin.

Boister did his own wetting down, but Jan declared he wasn't energetic enough in the application of the soap and ended up scrubbing him.

"My skin's gonna come off!" Boister declared as he turned pink under the scant bubbles of the lye soap.

The girls laughed, and Jan showed no mercy.

"Your turn," Boister declared as he hunkered by the fire in his blanket. His eye was on Tildie.

She turned pink, but declared, "Yes, I must have my turn. If you gentlemen will put up a blanket for privacy, Marilyn will help me."

"Me, too," insisted Evie. "Wash Tildie. I scrub, scrub, scrub-a-dub."

"You'll have to be gentle, Evie," Jan said, gazing at Tildie's blush. "Remember, your cousin got hurt and has been sick."

"You better let me do the scrubbing," said Mari, importantly. "You can wrap her in the blanket."

"Well then," said Tildie, thoroughly embarrassed. "Shall we get started?"

Her bath took a while and there was a lot of giggling behind the makeshift screen. Jan concentrated on keeping a fresh supply of water warm and studiously avoided watching the blanket being bumped by the figures behind it.

With all the bodies washed except Jan and Gladys, Tildie

instructed from her bed that their clothing must be washed. The dollies were set on the hearth to observe the proceedings as they, themselves, dried. With only the small bucket and kitchen kettle to use for washing, laundry was an all-afternoon project. During the process, Mari and Evie managed to get their cloth dolls soaking wet again, and they were laid farther from the hubbub of activity to dry.

The children were draped in their blankets with ropes binding their garments to them. Jan said they looked like Romans in togas and spent an hour explaining about the customs of early Greece and Italy while they labored over the soapy project. Tildie fell asleep directly after dinner which was cooked amidst garments hanging about, drying in the cabin's fireplace heat.

She awoke to a darkened room. The blanket still hung over the space in front of her bed. Jan was there straightening the pallet he slept on beside her. "Jan."

"Sorry, I didn't mean to wake you."

"I can't see you."

He leaned over the bed so his face was close to hers. She felt his nearness, but it was so dark she still couldn't see.

"It's snowing again," he said.

She touched the side of his face.

"Your hair's wet."

"I took a bath after the children were in bed."

"Thank you."

"Oh, you're welcome. I couldn't be the only human in the cabin who smelled." She could hear the laughter in his voice.

"No, I meant, thank you for going to all the trouble. For the children, for me."

"We're going to be here a long time, Tildie—maybe until spring. You can't travel now, and by the time you can, hard winter will have set in."

"Are we going to be all right? Is there enough food, enough fuel?"

He took her hand, the one with which she unconsciously stroked the side of his face, feeling the smoothness of his just shaved cheek.

"Yes, that's no problem. I'll hunt now, and we can dry the meat or let it freeze in the cave I use for storage. There are trees all around us for firewood. It may be difficult to get enough hay in for the stock, but I'll manage. It would be nice if we had a cow."

"A cow?"

"Milk and cheese for the little ones."

"The children will get bored."

"If they're bored, we'll give 'em baths. That took all day, and they loved running around in their togas, playing chase between the hanging clothes."

"Do you mind them?"

"Last year, I was nearly crazy with loneliness. No, I don't mind them." She liked his tone of voice. She could listen to him talk this way every night. It was nice to have him there.

"There is something else, Tildie." He sounded serious. Was he going to talk about her injuries? Did he have something to say about why it was taking her so long to recover?

"What?" she whispered in her anxiety.

"I don't think of you as one of the children. I think of you as a woman—a warm, beautiful, kind, sweet woman."

She started to cry.

It alarmed him. "I wouldn't hurt you, Tildie. I'd never do that, but it's going to be a long winter in this cabin, and I've got my heart set on marrying you."

"But I'm sick and maybe a cripple. . .and until today, I smelled like a goat."

"You're brave, and you're going to get well. And until today, I smelled like a buffalo."

She giggled through the tears.

"I don't know if I love you," she admitted. "Sometimes, I think I'd die if you walked away and left us. I've thought about when we get back to the ranch and you've fulfilled your promise to see us safely away from the Indians. Then, you'd leave us. I don't want that."

He stroked her hair back from her face, and she felt warm and secure.

"I've never been in love, Jan. I don't know if I can be a good wife. All I've thought about the last two years is keeping a roof over my head, then keeping the children safe and happy."

He kissed her then, interrupting her ramblings. When his lips released hers, she gasped a tiny little breath of air that tickled his lips so close to hers.

"Jan," she whispered.

"You talk too much." He kissed her again.

When he pulled away, he stared at her, barely making out her features in the dark.

"Do you think you could love me?" he asked.

"Yes." The answer came without hesitation. He smiled. He shifted, deliberately moving away from her but retaining her hand in his. He sat on his pallet with his back against the wall.

"We'll have to get married," he said huskily.

"How can we do that?"

"I'll marry us. When the spring comes, we'll register the wedding in the nearest town that has a courthouse. That may be clear back in Oklahoma. Can you handle that? We'll be married in the eyes of God. The children will be our witnesses. It's unusual, but out in the wilderness, that's how some couples have to do it."

"Have you married people before?" This thought fascinated her.

"Yes, I was a regular preacher before I came west to be a missionary."

"I didn't know that. Jan, there's an awful lot I don't know about you."

"We've got a long, cold winter ahead of us. By spring we

should be pretty well acquainted."

"When will we get married?"

"Let's say. . .when you're strong enough to stand up for the ceremony."

"How long do you think that will take?"

He rose up on his knees and came to kiss her again, trailing light, feathery kisses over her forehead, down her cheeks, and settling on her lips. He pulled himself away abruptly.

"Go to sleep now, Tildie. Rest, so you can get well quickly."

"Good night, Jan."

"Good night, Honey."

eleven

"A new parson came to the village parish," said Jan. From her bed, Tildie smiled at the thick Swedish accent he adopted for the telling of one of his grandmother's tales.

"He asked how there came to be in the church cemetery a lifelike, stone statue of a man of humble means. Why 'tis a man of two centuries past who, while walking through the grounds on a beautiful spring day, had the insensitivity to make a cruel remark regarding the dead. Instead of the proper respect, he said they'd done what they did in life to earn where they slept in death. He was instantly turned to stone, whereas his companion, who had doffed his hat, and said, 'God's peace to all who rest here,' marched on without feeling so much as a twinge in his overworked limbs."

"Limbs in a tree?" asked Mari.

"No, your arms and legs are limbs," explained Boister with scant tolerance for his little sister's ignorance. "Means he didn't have a charlie horse or cramp or nothing."

"Charlie? Horse?" Evie's big eyes turned toward the stable end of the cabin.

"Oh, forget it," said Boister at the end of his patience. "Tell the story, Jan."

"The parson said the statue should've been prayed over to release the poor, unfortunate man now that he had learned the error of his ways. The townsfolk said, indeed, the man had been prayed over by every parson since."

The wide-eyed children sat, listening to every word, Boister on his pallet with Gladys, Mari and Evie on their own. Jan sat in his chair between them, leaning forward as he told one of the many bedtime stories they indulged in every night.

"Well, the parson was a man who liked a challenge, so he had three strong men from the parish carry the stone statue and set it in the corner of his study where it would be within hearing of the many prayers he said each day.

"It was this parson's custom to end his evening prayers with these words, 'And by your grace, Heavenly Father, banish all that is evil from this house. Amen.' As the weeks went by, the parson began to think that there was a flurry of activity in the room each night after he said this prayer. It was nothing he could hear or see but rather a stirring of the air.

"He was a practical man who didn't worry too much about it, figuring if it was something beyond him to deal with, then his mighty God was taking care of it. One night he heard a small noise like a chuckle from the corner of the room where stood the statue. It was such a small tittering sound that he was not quite sure he heard it. The next night he heard it again, and it was more distinct. He took up his candle and peered about in the corner. Nothing, so he went to bed. The next night he heard it even more plainly, and since there was nothing in the corner besides the statue, he determined that it was the statue who had laughed.

" 'Now,' he says to the statue, 'If I can hear you laugh, then I can hear you talk. Be so kind as to tell me what makes you laugh each night.' Considering the state of the man in a statue-like pose, he thought there could not be much to laugh at."

"How can a statue talk?" asked Marilyn.

"It's a story," answered Boister. "Be quiet."

Jan continued. "The statue spoke very courteously to the parson. Remember, he has had a long time to repent of harsh words. He said that the parson was a very kind man, a very learned man, a very good counselor to his parishioners, and a very witty man behind the pulpit telling very worthy accounts from the Bible. However, he quarreled a little too much with his headstrong wife. 'Every night you call upon God to banish all evil from the house,' explained the voice from the statue, 'and a thousand little imps dance out the door. With each cross and contrary word which passes between wife and husband the next day, they come back in one by one.'

"The statue went on to explain that among these imps was a little fellow 'who wiggles about so, and does such tricks on his merry way out the door' that the statue could not help but laugh at his antics and funny faces.

"The parson had a heavy heart from hearing this. He went to his wife and explained that when stones began to speak in his study, it was wise for them to listen. They agreed to speak more kindly to one another and not be quick to anger, nor insensitive to each other's feelings.

"The wife was particularly unhappy to think of impish creatures free in her home throughout the day. Husband and wife behaved more seemly and soon began to enjoy each other as they had when first they were married.

"The statue was silent, and after many months when the parson and his wife were truly happy once again, the parson thought to ask the statue had he not seen the little imps, and particularly the one who made him laugh?

"The statue declared that he had upon occasion seen him lurking outside the door, peeping in, and being very impatient about it. The imp had finally given up and gone—no doubt to find a more quarrelsome household.

"The parson called his wife to rejoice with him, and thanked God together for ending their petty disagreements. The wife asked how it was with the statue, considering they were so happy and he was still stone.

"The statue replied that he was very nearly at peace, for he had done the kind parson a good deed. When the parson said his prayers that very night, the stone became flesh, drew his first breath in a three hundred years and his last throughout eternity. The parson and his wife saw that he had a very nice funeral, for they were glad of the man's release from his penance and grateful that their own entrapment in hasty words was ended."

"Tildie always says, 'and they lived happily ever after.' " Mari informed Jan. "That way we know the story is over and we have to lie down."

"Well, my grandmother never said it, but I don't think it will ruin her stories." Having told the story with the heavy Swedish accent, now that he was just talking, the inflection lingered upon his words. Tildie liked the sound of it, and she listened carefully as he continued. "The parson and his wife lived happily ever after. Now, put your heads on your pillows and go to sleep."

"Jan, do you tell your grandmother's stories to the Indians?" asked Boister.

"No, I only tell them stories from the Good Book. I think I might confuse them since they're just learning facts from the Bible. I wouldn't want them to expect to pray a person out of a stone statue."

"Don't you think we might get confused?" Boister asked. "I mean, I never would, but the little girls might."

"No, you don't have a language problem and are here to ask me or Tildie questions any time you want. Also, since you already know so much, it is good for you to use your brain and decide which is a fun story and which is the truth from God's Holy Word. You're a stronger Christian because you can think these things through."

"I want a kiss good night," declared Mari.

"Kiss, too," added Evie.

Before Jan could answer, the girls scrambled out of their covers and gave Jan a hug and kiss. They next stormed Tildie's bed, remembering just in time to carefully climb up instead of madly scrambling to kiss her. Jan watched them with a big grin on his face. When they came back, he knelt beside their pallet and carefully tucked them in, pausing to pray their good-night prayers with them.

He blew out the candle. Turning away, he was surprised to

find Boister standing beside him. He looked at the boy and saw there was something he wanted to say.

"Boister?" he inquired softly.

There was no response. Jan, who was still on his knees, leaned back so he sat on his heels. The flickering light from the fire revealed the little boy's features tightened in a mask of indecision. With an expelled breath of tension, Boister leapt at Jan, threw his arms around his neck, and gave him a quick, convulsive hug. Then just as quickly, he let go and darted across the room to dive into his blankets, turned his back to the room, and laid very still as if he had instantly gone to sleep.

Jan slowly rose to his feet and walked to the boy's pallet. He leaned over, pulled the blanket up more securely around his shoulders, then laid his big hand on the boy's small head for an instant. He said no words but across his face the look of tenderness Boister evoked was clearly evident. He moved then to settle on his pallet on the floor beside Tildie's bed.

After a few minutes, he reached up over the side of the bed to find Tildie's hand and hold it.

"Why are you sniffling?" he asked.

"I'm happy."

"Boister?"

"Yes, he's going to be all right. You've helped him where I couldn't. Thank God John Masters was taking us to Fort Reynald. Thank God for the accident. My aunt would have been happy to know that her son was better. She truly loved her children, you know. She was just incapable of fighting the circumstances. She gave up."

"We won't give up, Tildie. We have the strength of our Savior to draw upon."

"She did too, Jan. She just forgot to use it. I think she always counted on Uncle Henry to seek God, so she just benefited second hand from his strength. When he was gone, she had no personal connection to God."

"I don't want that to happen to you, Tildie. We must teach the children well."

"Yes, Jan." Tildie turned on her side and smiled into the darkness. She was happy with how God had changed her life. If asked to choose this road, she never would have taken it, not being able to see this place she had come to from the beginning. This, however, was good. She knew the truth of the verse which says all things work together for good to them who love God.

twelve

Tildie stood behind the chair, marveling that she was doing so without hurting. She let go and stood with her hands out to her sides.

"Very good," said a voice in back of her. She jumped and grabbed for the chair as she lost her balance. Strong arms caught her and swept her up. Jan held her against his chest. "Does this mean I finally have a bride?" He kissed her nose.

Tildie giggled. "Put me down. I want to try a step."

Boister, Mari, and Evie gathered around. Evie clapped her hands as Jan set Tildie on her feet and steadied her. When he let go she started to sink, so he wrapped his arms around her middle and stood close.

"Okay, Tildie, I'll support your weight, and you walk. Right foot first." She felt his right thigh pushing against the back of her right leg. She concentrated and managed to work with him, moving the heavy leg forward in a slow dragging step. For some reason, her toes didn't want to lift off the floor.

"Great. Now the other side," urged Jan.

Six steps and she was exhausted. He kissed the back of her ear as she slumped against him. "We've got all winter. Before spring we'll have you turned around, facing me, and we'll be dancing."

Tildie laughed softly at his optimism. He made it seem possible.

"Dancing!" Evie squealed.

"You don't even know what dancing is," scoffed Boister.

"She saw the Arapahos do the Sun Dance," said Mari in defense of her little sister.

"She never saw a square dance."

"You never saw a square dance either." Mari's jaw set in a defiant line.

"I did," said Boister. "You just don't remember."

"That's enough. You'll have little imps dancing all over the house with your contentious words." Jan's voice interrupted their debate. "Let me put your cousin in her chair, and I'll tell you an Arapaho Indian tale."

Boister pushed the chair they had padded with deer skins over closer to the fireplace, and the girls pulled their pallet over as well. Instead of placing Tildie in the chair, Jan sat in it and kept her in his lap.

"Many years ago, the buffalo left the Arapaho. The women of the Arapaho frowned with worry. The children of the Arapaho cried with hunger. The chiefs of the Arapaho turned to Black Robe, a medicine man of great power. Black Robe didn't have the magic to call the buffalo back to the plains without at least one buffalo to use his magic on. He decided to ask Cedar Tree for help and sent the mighty warrior west to hunt the buffalo.

"Cedar Tree hunted for many days and finally he saw black forms upon the horizon. He traveled eagerly toward what he hoped would be buffalo, but as he got closer, he began to doubt that he had found the buffalo. Then one of them spread wings and flew into the sky. Soon all the black forms sprouted wings. Clearly, they were ravens taking flight.

"Discouraged, Cedar Tree returned to the village and told Black Robe what he'd seen. The medicine man was greatly displeased.

" 'Don't you know, Cedar Tree, that you have been tricked by your own thoughts. You did see buffalo. If you had remained firm in your belief, you could have walked among them and slain the biggest to save our tribe from starvation. Instead, you let them trick you into thinking they were black birds. You allowed them to fly away.'

"The Arapaho village suffered. One old woman took off her moccasins and boiled them to make soup. Her uncle, Trying Bear, an even older Indian, did not like the taste of his dinner and set off to find something else to put in the pot. He was so old he did not even have weapons.

"Trying Bear passed Black Robe sitting on a rock. Black Robe gave the old man a bow and arrow and told him he was to hunt until he found something, even if it was only the carcass of a buffalo long dead with only scraps of dried flesh clinging to the bone.

"Trying Bear hunted a long time and did find a dried buffalo carcass. He had no need to shoot it with an arrow, so he shot the arrow straight into the sky in celebration. The arrow landed back in the camp and Black Robe knew the old man had found what was needed.

"Black Robe painted his black pony white because this was part of his magic. Many Arapaho warriors followed Black Robe because they wanted to see what he would do. The medicine man traveled until the sun was high in the sky, then he came upon Trying Bear waiting patiently beside the dead buffalo. Black Robe took his magic eagle feather and threw it, point first, into the bones of the dried buffalo. Immediately, a live buffalo rose out of the dead one.

"Black Robe turned to Trying Bear, impatient because the old man just sat there.

" 'Shoot it,' he commanded.

"Trying Bear shot it.

"Black Robe turned to the Arapaho who had followed him. 'Do you see the ravens flying down to land in the field beyond the hill? Go shoot the buffalo you find there.'

"The men went over the hill and found the buffalo that had so long hidden from them. There was a great feast of thanksgiving in the village lasting many days."

"Did they see the dead buffalo turn into the live one?" asked Boister.

"They said so," answered Jan.

"Is it real?" asked Mari.

"What do you think?" asked Jan.

Marilyn turned to her big brother for his verdict.

"Only God can do a miracle. It's a story."

Jan nodded. "What truth is in that story? Why tell it?"

Boister scrunched up his face while he thought. "If you want to help, you can help even if you aren't the best hunter. You have to do what you're told to do."

Jan smiled and roughed up Boister's hair. "Right, and I told those Indians who told me that tale that God has many stories in His Book that says that God uses the weak to dumbfound the mighty."

"Like Joshua," said Boister, "at the Battle of Jericho."

"And Gideon leading a handful of men to defeat an army," added Tildie.

"David," said Mari, "and Go-li-uff."

"Jesus," Evie said and clapped her hands.

"Yes," said Jan. "Even Jesus came as a poor baby, not a mighty warrior. That confused the Jews."

Evie stood up and went to stand beside Jan. She pushed at Tildie with her little hand.

"My turn," she said, sticking her lower lip out in a pronounced pout. "Tildie, get up!"

Jan laughed. "You don't really want to sit tamely in my lap." He stood up and gently placed Tildie in the chair. "Since Tildie can't dance yet, why don't you and I do a jig?"

He lifted the little girl into his arms and twirled her around the room while singing a lively song in Swedish. Boister grabbed Mari by the hands, and the two spun around and 'round, not really keeping step to the music.

Tildie clapped her hands and hummed along. Happy, she considered the many good times between them. Now, if she could only get up out of the chair and help more in the cabin.

Their days began to take on a routine. Jan carved shallow trays from a slab of wood and filled them with sandy dirt. Daily, Tildie taught the children to write their letters in the trays. Jan read from his books or told stories. Tildie exercised her legs with Jan's help, then with two crutches Jan and Boister made for her. Slowly, she gained enough strength to stand on her own and walk.

ò&

"I'm going down to Fort Reynald to get some supplies," Jan announced one night as they lay in bed, he on the pallet, and she on the pine needle mattress.

"How long will you be gone?" Tildie didn't like the idea, and a plaintive tone invaded her voice.

"About a week."

"Jan, what do we need so badly?"

"Flour, salt, and I'll try to get Christmas presents for the children. Maybe there'll be some material and you can make dresses for the girls."

"Is it really necessary?"

"I wouldn't leave if I didn't think so, and I trust you'll be all right. The weather's been so warm, there's little snow on the ground. It's best that I go now, while I still can." He reached up and patted her hand reassuringly. "Boister's become right handy. You're strong enough now almost to walk without those crutches. I'll even leave Gladys with you."

She grasped his hand. "Jan, come up here. Please. I don't want to talk to you when you're so far away."

"All of two feet."

"Please."

"No, Honey, it's *not* a good idea."

"Jan," she pleaded.

"Enough, Tildie. Be quiet, or I'll go to sleep with the horses."

"They'd step on you."

"As you're stepping on my heart right now. Don't ask such a thing of me, Tildie."

"I'm sorry."

He rose and gathered her in his arms to kiss her with all the longing that drove him crazy. He released her and sat back as far away from her as the tiny space would allow. "Do you understand, Tildie? I'll be wanting us to marry just as soon as I get back."

"I understand."

"I'm going to sleep out with Boister and Gladys." He quickly rolled up his pallet. "Goodnight, Honey."

"Goodnight, Jan."

❧

In the morning, they helped him get his things together. He readied Horse and Greedy Gert. He would ride on Gert and use Horse to pack out furs they had ready, but didn't need to use themselves.

He kissed Tildie and the girls good-bye, then gave Boister a sturdy hug. "Take care of them for me. If the weather turns bad, it may take me a little longer to return. You're not to worry, and don't let the women worry either."

Boister grinned, accepting the responsibility eagerly.

Jan rode off into the sunshine, following the path which led to a game trail down the mountain. The fine day begged Tildie to bring her chair outside, so they did their letters and sums in the dirt together. Evie drew pictures with her stick beside her older brother and sister. They were so peaceful in their endeavors that two chipmunks scampered on a log near the door with no fear.

Tildie gave thanks for the beauty that surrounded them and prayed safety for Jan.

thirteen

Established by fur traders, raucous Fort Reynald held not a single woman within its walls. Situated on the Arkansas River at the best ford for miles up or down the river, it catered to the rugged mountain men and traded with Indians for buffalo skins.

Jan went to trade his furs at the long, low shack with the hand-scrawled sign claiming, "Mercantile." He found brightly colored material for the girls' dresses. Since the Indians favored the pretty calicoes, the dealer had a good variety. Jan got plenty to make the girls' dresses and maybe a shirt for Boister. He also bought a rifle, intending to take the boy hunting.

The owner also had an assortment of oddities gathered when the mountain men traded for supplies. Jan looked them over, searching for a ring to surprise Tildie when they wed. There was none. He bought a knife for Boister, a hair ornament worked in leather for Marilyn, and a little copper pot with a lid for Evie. He bought enough forks and spoons so all of them could have their own when they sat down to dinner. They'd been using wooden spoons that he had whittled.

One spoon stood out among all the others. It was obviously silver with a slender handle and a floral design at its end. Although tarnished, Jan knew it would serve the function he had in mind. He smiled as he added it to his selections.

Next, he went over to the side of the building which stored the grocer goods.

"You be the preaching Swede, be you not?" asked a man with a thick French accent. He sat on a barrel behind the counter, his feet propped up on a stack of boxes marked "salt."

A heavyset man, not fat, his short frame bulged with massive muscles. His dark beard straggled from a swarthy face. His greasy hair matched his old, worn clothes in filth. He'd whittled a toothpick and passed it back and forth across his row of yellowed teeth as he spoke.

Jan looked into the small, shifty eyes of Armand des Reaux. "My name's Jan Borjesson. I've traded here before."

"Heard you lived with the Indians." The grocer's voice held a note of disdain.

"I've lived with several tribes."

"Arapaho?" Des Reaux spit out the word.

"Yes."

"You being an Indian-lover, I suppose they'd give you something valuable if it came their way?"

"I don't know what you mean?"

"A white woman, say a young white woman." Des Reaux rose from his seat and leaned menacingly over the makeshift counter.

His attitude drew the attention of the men swapping tales around the pot-bellied stove. They stopped to listen to the exchange at the counter. Many of them had heard des Reaux brag about how his bed would be warmed this winter.

"I've just collected my family from Chief Two Bear's camp. Is that what you're referring to?" Jan responded quietly, seemingly undisturbed by the questions.

Des Reaux snorted. "Seems improbable a man who lives in the mountains, travels over the plains living with Injuns, does a little fur trading on the side, should all of a sudden acquire a wife and three shavers."

The dirty Frenchman shrugged as if he was merely relating an interesting bit of speculation, but Jan knew better. Menace underlined every word.

"Now, I was expecting a bride this summer," continued des Reaux. He stood polishing one of the many knives from his display case. "She was being brought to me by a friend." He paused and looked directly at Jan. "A friend who never made it."

Des Reaux carefully put the knife down and picked up a bigger, wicked looking blade before he spoke again. "I traded with Drescher a while back, and he's friendly with your Arapaho."

Jan nodded. "I know Drescher."

"He tells me that the Arapaho took on a young white woman with three kids. This most unusual event happened just about the time my bride was to come. Very unusual, don't you think?"

"My friend Moving Waters," Jan said distinctly, "came to get me. He recognized whose family had come to their camp."

"Not many white women in this territory." The words dismissed Jan's explanation as if he hadn't even spoken. The Frenchman suddenly leaned back, but rather than easing the tension, the move charged the air. In the same way a mountain lion drawn back to spring on his prey flexes his muscles, he turned the knife in his hand over and over in a rhythmic motion.

"Was your bride bringing you three children to rear?" asked Jan.

"Maybe yes, maybe no." Des Reaux sneered.

"And, the name of your bride?" asked Jan, wondering just how much the man knew about John Masters' niece.

Des Reaux's eyes narrowed with hatred. "What would be the name of this woman you got from the Arapaho?"

"Tildie. The children are Henry, Marilyn, and Evelyn. Have you any more questions before we get around to the salt, flour, salt pork, and beans I came for?"

Des Reaux reached behind him and Jan tensed for action, but the Frenchman merely put down the knife and pulled out a pad of paper, slamming it down on the counter top.

"I don't know you. I'll want hard cash for your goods." The words delivered implied an insult but Jan ignored them and got down to the business of acquiring the things he wanted. The grocer scratched out the charges on his paper and totaled the sum.

It seemed high to Jan, and he asked to see the list. The men behind him once more abandoned their talk to watch the next episode. A fight would relieve the monotony.

Jan found an error in addition and pointed it out. He was on the alert. The Frenchman might have made an honest mistake, but it was more likely he meant to cheat him or provoke a fight. Des Reaux shook his head and smiled. Somehow the smile was not reassuring.

"I have made a mistake. We all make mistakes. Is it not so, Monsieur? Some mistakes, however, are more costly than others."

Jan felt a frisson of warning and prayed that God's angels would protect him from this wicked man, for now Jan was sure that the trader was not merely unpleasant, but truly evil. He prayed to be alert to the danger and ready to protect himself. The Frenchman was plotting some revenge. Even if he was unsure that Jan had taken the woman he planned to marry, he hadn't liked being pointed out in error over the bill.

Jan took his purchases to one of the outer buildings where he expected to spend the night. Still within the compound of the fort, the boardinghouse had several rooms where lodgers slept side by side on the floor. After looking over the accommodations, he decided to sleep with the horses in the livery. The bedding was filthier than the last time he'd been in Reynald, and he didn't wish to itch all night and carry bed bugs back with him.

"Now, I don't mind the company," said the young man who ran the stable. His speech more formal than the usual in the west. He delivered it with great precision and a thick British accent, "But I'll be charging you for the stall just as if you put another horse in here."

Jan laughed, for the small Englishman had a cocky smile

on his unlined face and was friendlier than most of the inhabitants of Reynald. He was by far cleaner, as well, than the old codgers around the fort.

"I don't mind paying. The hay here is cleaner than the blankets at the house."

"I've been told that before. It might not be as warm here as it is in the house, but few of the horses snore."

"My name is Jan Borjesson. I don't believe you were here the last time I was through."

"My name's Henderson. I came to the territory in late March, and now I shall most likely reside here forever." He sighed as if admitting a great sorrow in his life.

"Why is that?" asked Jan, intrigued by the man's sudden gloom.

"Have a seat, and I'll tell you a sad story."

Jan pulled up a small, empty nail barrel, sat down, and leaned back against the stall door where Greedy Gert ate her dinner. He noted that the Englishman had perked up at his interest and didn't look particularly despondent about the prospect of telling his sad tale.

"Cup of tea?" Henderson offered.

"Thanks." Jan took the warm mug of strong, sweetened tea.

"My story starts in London. I was the butler to the Earl of Dredonshire as was my father before me. The earl died and the new earl was a bit of a scoundrel. I had it in my mind that I didn't want to settle down to the same life my father had. I decided to cross the Atlantic and start fresh in a new country.

I was seasick to the point of offering fellow passengers all my worldly goods if they'd just end my life in a quick and painless way. One more day at sea, and there would have been no need to employ their services."

"Can't say I've ever been plagued with that particular ailment," commiserated Jan. "Of course, I've never been on the ocean—just Lake Erie."

"Please, let us not mention any body of water bigger than a mud puddle."

Jan laughed.

"I lay torpid—"

"Torpid?" Jan interrupted.

"Oh, definitely torpid, dear sir," said the ex-butler.

Jan saw the gleam of subtle humor in the young Englishman's eye and liked him better for it.

"I lay torpid in New York City," Henderson began again, "until I could stand once more. Then, I felt the inclination to come deeper into the country. I heard of prairies so wide, you could walk days and not come across another human."

Jan nodded for that was certainly true.

"Unfortunately, I got sick on the train. Indeed, it was not as bad as when I was on the ship, but my constitution just isn't made for traveling.

"Next, I rode in a wagon. I surmised that that conveyance would be slower and wouldn't cause me much discomfort." The Englishman shook his head mournfully. "A wagon proved to be irrevocably and too frequently plagued by great jostling. I decided a horse might prove acceptable to my contrary stomach. This, too, proved to be disastrous.

"Mr. Borjesson, I *walked* the last three hundred miles to this fort, and I am ashamed to say I was stricken with yet another malady."

"Surely, you weren't nauseated while walking?" Jan asked incredulously.

Henderson stared down at his boot tips and sighed wearily. "No, I discovered a phobia, a weakness of character, that has doomed me to stay within the confines of this rudimentary settlement."

"Rattlesnakes?" guessed Jan, thoroughly understanding how one could be terrified of the venomous beasts.

"No," said Henderson wearily. "Perhaps you will understand if you know a little of my background. I was born in

London. Never traveled until the day I set out for America. The most grass I'd seen at one time was in the London parks. The aristocrats prefer beautifully kept, tidy bits of lawn. Groomed, you might say, to match the cosmopolitan style of the populace.

"On the ship, I rarely came above deck. Those few times I did, the sight of the expanse of ocean quickly heaved my stomach. In New York, there were buildings to which I was accustomed. On the train, I rarely looked out the window since the countryside speeding by adversely affected my internal organs.

"I rode inside the wagon, and I stayed mounted on the horse for less than a day. At this point, I was bound to my companions by the sheer circumstance that I could *not* return east on my own, not knowing anything about the country or how to survive. For weeks I walked in utter agony, every moment fighting as panic rose within my breast, threatening to drive me mad. Once within these wooden barricades, I was able to resume a more equable demeanor."

"I don't understand," said Jan. "Were you afraid of Indians, wild beasts, renegades?"

"The open space, Mr. Borjesson. The great endless expanse. The complete infinity of the horizon. It is a completely irrational fear. Totally beyond my abilities to subdue."

fourteen

Jan watched the Englishman's display of total dejection. The man used a great deal of self-effacing humor in the telling of his tale, but there was an underlying melancholy that rang true. Jan tried to imagine the grip of such a terror and found it difficult. To fear being out in the open? Preposterous!

Of course, he knew many a man who broke out in a cold sweat at the sound of a rattler. Jan, himself, got a chill up his spine whenever he encountered a snake. He didn't particularly like scaling cliffs, either. . .but to be paralyzed with dread? The closest he could recall being in that kind of panic was when he thought Tildie might slip out of his grasp into the torrential waters of the flash flood.

Henderson jumped up, startling Jan. "Enough of this! They tell me you are a family man, and des Reaux has taken a dislike to you."

"I did get that impression," agreed Jan.

"Not an enviable place to be," sympathized the Englishman. "Des Reaux is a frustrated man and therefore, dangerous. He does not have the power over the fur traders he imagined when he embarked on this enterprise."

"How do you know this?" asked Jan.

"The Frenchman drinks, and when he drinks, he talks. Since no man is his friend, he comes out to the livery and talks to his mule. A very sad state of affairs, don't you think?"

Jan nodded his agreement, noting again the humor on Henderson's face.

"Des Reaux is disappointed to have a man of integrity sharing his place of business. Across the room, Rodgers, in the mercantile, will not cooperate in the Frenchman's schemes to turn a bigger profit. Des Reaux is affronted daily by the gall of honesty.

"And des Reaux ran a saloon in St. Joe. He misses the excitement. Unfortunately, he had to leave that establishment quickly. A situation turned sour over the lamentable death of one of his clients.

"A particularly unpleasant part of his exile is the lack of female companionship, and he thought that rectified. Something went wrong. The white female was not delivered. He advanced fifty dollars to an imbecile—this is the word he uses—eager for the supplies. Des Reaux made an error in judgement.

"The Frenchman is a dangerous man because he is angry over too many things. His life is full of irritations."

"You're saying the Frenchman bought a wife."

Henderson shrugged, "An arranged marriage. I tell you, his heart was not engaged. He was discussing the woman with his mule one night, and he could not even remember her name. Only that it started with an M—Mary, Martha, Melissa, Margaret. He guessed them all, and none sounded right to his intoxicated brain."

The Englishman sat abruptly on a bale of hay.

"Now," he said, "you have heard too much about me and too much about the despicable des Reaux. I am interested in you. Do I discern in you a kindred spirit? I have heard of you, the Swedish preacher who lives among the Indians. Tell me of your adventures. I may never walk out onto the plains again, but you shall free me in my mind. I shall see the things you have seen. I shall know those whom you have known."

"That's a pretty tall order."

"First then, tell me of the friends you have made among the Indians. They fascinate me."

The two men enjoyed each other's company and talked late into the night. Henderson shared his dinner with Jan and gave him an extra blanket to put between him and the itchy straw. In the morning, they continued their discussion while Henderson used his small forge to fashion the silver spoon handle into a ring, a Christmas present for Tildie.

Jan thought it was worthwhile to remain an extra day. Henderson began questioning what the preacher told the Indians and the opportunity arose to share the gospel with this displaced English butler.

"Henderson, you're needed over at the boarding house." A rough looking trader interrupted their talk in the early morning.

"What is it?"

"Knifing."

"You must excuse me, Jan," apologized the livery man. "I have some skill in taking care of wounds and am called upon at least twice a week to stitch up someone, pull a tooth, or remove a bullet. Please stay. I shall return as soon as is possible."

Henderson returned an hour later and busied himself about the livery taking care of chores. Jan joined him, helping out where he could.

"My suspicions have been aroused over this knifing," admitted Henderson. "There was no reason for the attack. No one knew of any grudge against the victim. He was a man who has often slept in one of the rooms, but this night he chose to sleep in a different room because he was finally, 'fed up' were the words he used, with a fellow boarder's snoring. He was the new man in a room usually given to those who do not sleep there for more than one night."

"I don't see what you're getting at, Henderson."

"Your disagreement with the French grocer. Of course, I admit to a healthy English prejudice against all things French, but Jan, the man who was knifed was of the same build as you. A very tall, lean giant of a man. Not as young or with hair as fair, but in the dark this would be indiscernible."

"You think des Reaux was out to murder me?"

"Oh, he would not have gone himself, but he is a disreputable villain."

"I can't take this seriously, Henderson. How could the man profit by my death?"

"To some, it is not always necessary to profit monetarily. He may believe that your lovely Tildie is his lost betrothed. You have therefore cheated him. Too, he did not care for your easy detection of the extra profit he hoped to make by misrepresenting your bill. Such a man would relish revenge even of an imagined insult."

"I think you're being highly dramatic, Henderson." Jan raised his hand to ward off Henderson's sputtering objection. "I'll watch my back, and I thank you for the warning, but I'm not convinced that an innocent man was stabbed because he happened to be lying in a place where I *might* be sleeping."

Henderson was slightly affronted by the disregard of his supposition. He became a very haughty Englishman for all of ten minutes, and Jan got a glimpse of how very proper an English butler could be. Henderson thawed in a short time.

Late in the evening, after several hours of spiritual talk, Henderson admitted his need for a Savior and bowed his head in submission and acceptance of the Master's plan.

The following morning, Jan presented him with a gift. Jan tore a few pages out of an old Bible.

"I'm tearing out the book of Acts, Henderson. I'm sorry but I've already ripped out the gospels and given them away. You'll find much to think on from this account of the young church. Here's an address you can write to, and the good people I know there will send you a whole Bible."

"Thank you, Jan." The Englishman held the pages carefully.

Jan swung up into the saddle and, with a promise to see Henderson at the next opportunity, bid the man farewell.

"Watch your back, Mr. Borjesson," Henderson said as he waved good-bye. "It is an American expression which I think is very apropos to your situation."

Jan grinned over the prim and proper young man's concern.

Two hours later he was no longer amused. He lay beside the trail with both horses gone, pressing his wadded up shirt to a bullet hole in his shoulder.

On the plus side, he wasn't so far from the fort that he couldn't walk back. On the minus side, the bushwhacker had hit him twice, once in the shoulder and a crease along his scalp. He had bound the head wound with his bandana, but it bled profusely and was slow to stop. The other bullet lodged in his shoulder and, if he was not mistaken, had broken his collarbone.

Jan leaned against the rock and wished some of his gear had fallen off the horse when he had. A canteen would be nice. The new rifle he'd purchased for Boister would be handy.

He reached in his pocket and retrieved his pocket knife. First cutting the sleeves off of his shirt, he rewadded the already soaked shirt and tied it on tight against the bullet hole. Next, he dragged himself over to what little shade an outcrop of rock and straggly scrub brush provided. He knew he was near collapse and didn't want to wake up in worse shape. Even though the winter sun didn't have the strength to fry him, lying unconscious beneath it at this altitude would be two more strikes against his chance of survival.

When he came to, the sun had disappeared behind the Rockies. The evening sky was still light, having taken on the aquamarine hue that would deepen to purple before the tiny pinpoints of starlight showed. The air had taken on a distinct chill and it helped clear his head.

Jan grimaced as he pulled himself to a sitting position. He maneuvered himself to sit on one of the lower rocks and looked about him for anything which would help. Jan reached out to pluck the old stems of a mountain dandelion. The dried plant could be chewed like gum, and he needed the little nourishment it would provide.

It wasn't cold enough for him to freeze to death during the night, but he would certainly lose energy staying warm. He'd had a rest, and it probably behooved him to make progress toward the fort while he could. Jan plucked another stem and searched around for a stick to make some kind of crutch. He found one long enough to use as a cane. It was better than nothing.

Closing his eyes, Jan prayed before he hoisted his considerable frame to his feet and started the trek back to the relative safety of the fort. He owed an apology to Henderson for scoffing at his concern and hoped he'd be able to deliver it.

Think, he ordered himself. *You've got to think straight, or you won't get out of this.* Sitting down before he fell down, Jan rested on a boulder. His mind drifted.

It had been a couple of hours, as near as he could figure. He'd concentrated on keeping his right shoulder to the mountains, not wanting to get turned around and lose time wandering.

Where was Camel Rock? Did he cross that stream by the stand of blue spruce? Jan swiped a shaky hand across his face. *All the landmarks couldn't have been swallowed up by the night. Am I passing them without seeing them? Am I lost?*

Oh, Father, guide my steps.

Jan moved on, forcing each foot to step forward as it came its turn.

Again, he slumped against an incline. It had been necessary to sit. For some time, he'd been fighting the dizziness. It wouldn't be wise to fall hard upon his shoulder and start the bleeding once again. With an effort, he formed words of a prayer in his head. He needed strength. He needed guidance. He needed endurance. He needed help. Fleetingly, he thought how desperately he needed to get back to Tildie and the children before winter set in—but that was trouble for another day. Tonight, he needed to stay alive.

The morning birds brought him back to his senses. Shivering, he struggled to his feet. He must make a few miles before he ground down to a complete halt. One foot in front of the other. One step at a time.

fifteen

If watching out the window could bring him back, thought Tildie, *Jan would be drawn here like a moth to the lantern.* She turned from the window and hobbled across to the table where the children shaped biscuit dough into odd clumps to drop in the fat to fry.

"That's too big, Boister," Mari said with authority. She often did kitchen chores with Tildie and felt that in this one area she had an advantage over her older brother. Since the last deep snow, Boister had joined them out of boredom.

"It'll be all soft and gooshy in the middle, even if the outside is nice and crisp." Mari continued to display her superior knowledge.

"I like the middle doughy," claimed Boister. He set his lump of dough aside and pinched off another.

"Snake," proclaimed Evie enthusiastically as she put her long piece with those to be fried.

"That's nothing but a fat worm," taunted Boister.

"You let imps in the house all the time," said Mari with a fierce scowl at her brother. "Remember Jan's story. There's no need to be ugly to Evie. Her snakes are as good as your great lumps that'll never cook through."

Tildie drew out the chair and sat down at the table. She laid her crutches on the floor. She could get by in the morning without using them, but they became necessary as the day wore on and she got tired. It irked her, and she deliberately turned to distract the children from their quarrel in hopes it would also distract her from the pain in her back that ran through her hip and down the right leg. Tildie picked up a lump of dough.

"They say in Africa there are animals as big as a house. They're called elephants and the only thing about them that is a normal size is their tail. An elephant has a tail much like a cow, only it is stuck to a body as big as this room." She fashioned a huge lump and stuck on a tiny tail.

"His legs are like tree trunks." She added four sturdy legs.

"He has a great, huge head, but tiny eyes." She picked up another pinch of dough, shaping the head and putting indentations for the eyes. "And he has flapping ears on each side of his head." The children giggled at the creature she held in her hand. "But the strangest thing is his nose, which comes out and out and out." She pulled and pinched until she had a trunk formed. "He can use it to pick up things, squirt water he sucks up from the river, or pat his baby elephant on the head."

"Can we fry him?" asked Boister.

"No, he'd fall apart," said Tildie. "I'm not as good as God at making wondrous creatures. Mine won't hold up under wear and tear."

"It isn't a real animal anyway," said Boister.

"Oh, but it is," declared Tildie. "Maybe it's the animal the Bible refers to as the behemoth or the leviathan."

"I thought that was a water animal," said Boister.

"Maybe, it is. I'm not sure." Tildie looked doubtfully at the elephant. She stood it on the table, and the weight of his body caused the legs to buckle. His head fell forward and was in danger of dropping off.

"I wish Jan were here. He would know," Mari sighed.

"He won't come back now," Boister announced. "Not 'til the snow melts."

"Is that true, Tildie? Is Jan not coming back?" Mari turned to her cousin and her eyes reflected the fear she was feeling. "Will he never come back? Will he come when the snow melts? Will he come at all?" The questions tumbled one after the other in an avalanche of apprehension. The last word came out with a sob.

Tildie reached across and gathered Mari in her arms, dropping bits of dough and shedding flour down her dress.

"He'll come back as soon as he can, Mari, as soon as he can."

"What if he fell off like Mama and. . ." she choked on the thought.

"He's used to traveling alone. He can take care of himself. He'd want us to be brave and look after ourselves, too. We can do that," said Tildie. She leaned away from the little girl. Still disregarding her floured hands, she took Mari's face between her palms. "We can do that, can't we?" Tildie looked the girl straight in the eye.

Mari stared back for a moment to gather the strength Tildie hoped she saw there. Nodding her head firmly, Mari answered, "Yes, we can!"

When the darkness came and the children were sound asleep the confidence that Tildie had manufactured for them disappeared. She lay in the bed Jan had given her and cried quietly, praying through the tears that her big Swede was not hurt, suffering someplace out on the trail. It never occurred to her that he might have just decided he didn't want a wife and family. She knew something had happened, because Jan Borjesson had promised to come back—and so far, he hadn't.

Mentally, she took stock of what provisions they had in the cabin. They could make it. With only one horse to feed instead of three, there was probably enough of the long meadow grass stacked for hay in the crib outside. Of course, they would have to stretch out the flour by making biscuits every other day. Would that be enough? Maybe she should say twice a week. The meat would last a long time, but they had no vegetables. Water was no problem, either. They had meat and water.

It might not be a very interesting diet, but they could live on it. They could live on it until Jan came back, and he would come back. He was not dead, just delayed. The very thought of him being dead caught at her heart, and she refused to entertain the notion.

The wind began to howl. Surely it was mocking her fears, trying to make her scream with terror. She would not! She would pray and be strong. God had seen her through the weeks at the Indian camp. God would be with her now.

It was a daily struggle. There wasn't enough to do to ward off the gnawing consternation. She invented things to keep busy. The children learned verses from the Bible. They acted out parts of the books Jan had on his bookshelf. They made up a song to learn Boister's addition and subtraction facts. Soon Mari, and even Evie, could sing facts from one plus one to nine minus nine. Tildie made up a story about a happy little imp who tried to steal ideas from them which they could use to keep from getting bored.

And Tildie walked. She paced back and forth in the little cabin, strengthening her legs. She'd march with the children, singing their numbers song and singing the songs her own father had sung when he sawed wood back in Indiana. In the back of her mind was the possibility that come springtime, she and the children would have to walk out of the mountains by themselves.

They'd just be going down to find Jan. It wasn't that he wasn't there. He wasn't dead. He couldn't come to them, but they would go to him. They just had to pass the time 'til the spring thaw. It was only a matter of time. *Oh, dear God, let it only be a matter of time.*

She wasn't tired enough. That was the problem. The little they did to occupy their time wasn't enough to wear her out so that when she laid her head down at night she could sleep.

Boister shoveled out the stall, kept Charlie provided with a clean stable, and brought in the hay for feed. Boister also took Charlie out into the yard and gave his little sisters rides, exercising the horse and pleasing the girls to no end. Boister brought in the wood, hauled out the ashes, and trudged through the snow with Gladys to the cave where meat was stored.

Tildie genuinely praised him for his efforts. Without him, she and the girls would be uncomfortable to say the least. Finally, Boister acted more like a normal boy, showing pride over his responsibilities, grumbling at his little sisters, and affectionately hugging Tildie when the notion struck him. She thanked God for rescuing Boister from that false guilt.

Many times when the sun shone, Tildie bundled up the children and let them roll snowballs to make snowmen in front of the cabin. She could only sit by the door. Her crippled legs couldn't forge through the snow.

How she would love to be so tired that she would sleep as soon as she crawled under the heavy blanket! She delayed going to bed. Once she lay down on that pine needle mattress, her mind began to churn. All the suppressed fears raised their ugly heads and hissed at her in the dark. The prayers she said in the morning to help her face the day sounded hollow and meaningless at night. . .and the nights were so long.

She hadn't conserved the candles until too late. She realized that the oil in the lamps wouldn't last forever, that the candles wouldn't burn all winter. They started to keep the candles and the lantern for special occasions and spent most of their time in what light the fire provided. Jan probably could have told her to be more careful. Jan would have known how to make more candles, but he wasn't here.

Then the noises began. It wasn't her imagination. Charlie shifted nervously in his stall. He whinnied his uneasiness. Gladys came awake and crouched next to the wall, growling in her throat. Outside, something clawed at the shutters, at the door, at the wall. For what seemed like hours, it wandered outside the cabin, coming back again and again to scrabble at the wood. Boister woke and came to sit in the bed with Tildie. Neither spoke. Perhaps if it didn't hear anything, it would go away.

In the morning, they looked at the tracks in the snow. They examined the deep claw marks in the soft pine wood around the door and windows.

"Do you know what that track is?" asked Tildie.

"Maybe bear," guessed Boister. "Jan never showed me that track, or I'd know."

"I thought bears slept through the winter," said Mari.

"Hibernate," said Tildie, "yes, bears hibernate."

"It's big," said Evie.

"Must be a bear," said Boister.

"Well, we'll just have to pray that bear goes to bed real soon." Tildie ushered her little tribe back into the cabin.

"He's been in the meat," Boister whispered to her that afternoon when he came in with a load of wood.

"We have Jan's rifle, and you can trap a rabbit. We won't starve, Boister—even if the bear eats all the meat. God will take care of us."

The bear was back again that night. He returned every night, and as Tildie examined the damage he did on the windows, she wondered how long it would be before he broke through.

Now she lay awake with new fears. She'd wait for the clawing to begin. Sometimes it was long in coming. She would think that he would skip a night, but just as she was drifting off, the persistent clawing began. She prayed that the thick walls and door would hold against the onslaught. She knew if the bear was in a rage, he could probably force his way in.

Every morning they surveyed the incredible damage, but the bear didn't seem intent on entering the cabin. Every night, he toyed with the windows and doors. Every night, either before or after, he would raid the cave and haul away some of the frozen meat.

One day Gladys roamed away from the cabin and didn't return.

"I've got to find her, Tildie. Jan left me in charge of taking care of you. That includes Gladys. Gladys is special. She's been Jan's dog forever. Jan will be so angry with me that she's gone."

Tildie had a hard time convincing Boister that he couldn't take off at dusk and search for the missing dog.

"Jan will understand. He'd be much madder if you did something you knew to be foolish. Going out in the dark on this mountain with a bear prowling about is foolish! Gladys has lived in the wilderness a lot longer than we have, and she probably knows more about how to take care of herself than we do."

"But she could be hurt someplace," protested Boister.

"I know," said Tildie softly, looking off towards the woods, wishing the dog would suddenly come bounding towards them.

"Jan won't be mad, Boister. He wouldn't lay the responsibility on you for what Gladys got in her head to do. Maybe she decided he's been gone too long, and she's gone off to find him."

"Do you really think so?" asked Boister.

Tildie shook her head. "I don't know what to think, except she's a pretty smart old dog. We just have to hope nothing bad has happened to her."

Gladys didn't return the next day. In looking for the old dog, Tildie suspected Boister explored as far away from the cabin as he dared.

The dog was a link to Jan. She'd been a comfort in one way or another to each member of the family. She went with Boister whenever he ventured outdoors. She lay with the girls when they took their naps or were playing quietly on their pallets, and she acted as a watchdog giving Tildie a confidence she needed. Now, with Gladys not around to bark her warnings, Tildie was even more concerned. They all missed her terribly, and the little girls cried at the loss of their friend.

sixteen

If she had Boister haul the meat into the cabin, would the bear become more determined to break in? They gathered up a good deal of the meat and hung it in bags of skin from branches high in a Ponderosa pine. The bear could climb as high as Boister. Three days after they'd hidden the stash, the bear discovered it. Boister thought maybe he'd followed his scent to the tree. Tildie admitted they didn't know enough about bears to even guess what was going on in the animal's head. All they could do was pray, and she didn't admit to the children how futile the exercise seemed to her.

A sunny day enticed them outside. Although the temperature was low, the high, dry mountain air made it almost comfortable. Tildie sat in the door of the cabin with mending in her hands. It was easier to stitch out in the sunlight than by the light of the fire. The girls strapped their dolls to flat pieces of wood they used as miniature sleds. Climbing up the small embankment, they let their dollies ride down, squealing as if they were the ones enjoying the sensation of speeding down the hill.

Maybe Tildie and Boister could rig up some kind of sleigh for the girls' Christmas present. Tildie mulled over the possibilities. Boister was out in the woods now, gathering what he recognized as edible. Tildie marveled at how much he'd learned while they spent the few months in the Indian village. He must have listened as well as watched for he brought things home from his foraging that the Indians had told him about but never shown him.

Shouting in the distance brought Tildie's head up. She rose to her feet. Was it Jan returning? No! As the hullabaloo came nearer, she caught the distress of Boister's shouts. The sound brought fear to her heart, clamping the muscles in her chest until she almost stopped breathing. She peered into the trees but could see nothing from the direction of his frantic yells.

"Get inside," Tildie ordered the girls, but they both froze. "Mari, Evie, inside, now!"

Evie started to cry, and Mari ran over to take her hand, trying to pull her towards the door. Evie sat down, still crying, and Mari started crying with her.

Boister broke through the last few bushes and started across the open space to the cabin. Behind him lumbered the bear. Tildie pushed the chair aside and rushed into the cabin to grab Jan's rifle. She'd never shot a gun before, but now was not the time to debate over whether she could or not. She ran out again.

Tildie raised the gun to her shoulder. She sighted down the barrel and squeezed the trigger. The explosion knocked her off her feet and back into the cabin. She lay there for a second with the smoking gun beside her. As she sat up, Boister came through the door with wailing Evie under his arm. Mari screeched as she followed him. Boister yelled to close and bar the door. Over the commotion the children made, Tildie could hear the roar of the angry bear.

Tildie scrambled out of the way as Boister threw Evie into her lap. Mari pushed at the door while Boister grabbed the bar. As he put his shoulder to the door and swung it shut, Tildie saw the bear within feet of entering the cabin. She pushed Evie off her lap and hurled herself against the door with Mari and Boister. The boy jammed the bar in place, and they all froze in their positions against the door.

Nothing happened. Evie cried loudly. Mari sobbed as she gasped for air. Tears rang down Boister's cheeks, and he panted from his long run. Tildie slid to the floor, still leaning heavily against the plank door.

There was no assault upon the door. No pounding, no

clawing, no enraged bear growling and snarling to get in. Where was he? Tildie looked at the window where both the inside shutters and outside shutters stood open.

She touched Boister's arm and pointed. He understood immediately and scrambled over to close and bar the shutters. He moved quickly to the two other windows, and then to the stable door. When all was secure, he came back to Tildie's side and sat down next to her.

"Are you hurt?" she asked as he moved as close to her as he could. Evie crawled across the floor and over Boister to get into Tildie's lap. "Are you hurt?" she repeated.

"No." His denial caught on a sob. He turned his face into her shoulder, and she knew he was crying quietly. His fists tightened on her sleeve, but he couldn't bring himself to speak. Tildie squeezed his shoulders and turned to the girls. "Mari, are you okay?"

Mari paused in her whimpering to nod. She sniffed and rubbed her nose on her sleeve. "Where is he?"

"I don't know," answered Tildie.

Evie reached up and put a little hand on Tildie's cheek. "Okay?" she asked. Her little face was tear-streaked, her eyes red from crying.

"Yes," Tildie laughed softly, "I'm okay, are you?"

Evie smiled and nodded. The tension eased from their bodies, and Mari gave a nervous giggle. "I was scared," she admitted.

"Me, too," Evie said and gave her sister a comforting pat.

Boister shuddered next to Tildie.

"We were all scared," said Tildie. "Boister was the bravest of all. He got us all into the cabin and barred the door."

"We all helped," said Mari.

Boister lifted his face and scrubbed at his eyes and cheeks. Evie stretched out her arms to him, and he grabbed her, holding her tight against his small chest. Mari crawled across Tildie to hug both of them. For a moment the four of them embraced in a family hug until Tildie spoke softly. "I have to get up off the floor. I don't know how much damage I did when I fell, but I'm beginning to hurt."

The children clambered off. Boister and Mari helped her rise and move awkwardly to the chair by the table. Evie helpfully pushed from behind.

The children stood close around her. Tildie sat in the chair, panting over the exertion. Mari reached over and took her big brother's hand. "Where did the bear go, Boister?"

Evie looked up at him, waiting for him to say. Tildie put a hand on his shoulder. "We have to look," she said quietly.

He nodded. Mari handed Tildie her crutches, and they moved solemnly to the front window. They stood in the dim light, listening. . .but heard no sound other than the wind from outside.

"Maybe we should load the gun again," suggested Boister.

Tildie nodded, and Boister ran to pick it up. He took care as he loaded it just as Jan had shown him.

"Girls, stand back," he ordered as he handed the rifle to Tildie. They scurried over to their pallet, and Tildie stood a few feet back as she aimed the gun at the window. Boister quietly pulled up the bar and lowered it to the floor. He eased one shutter open a crack and peered through.

He shut it and turned back to Tildie.

"I don't see anything."

"Listen," she instructed. "Maybe you'll hear him."

Boister opened the shutter a crack again and listened. He opened it wider and looked with more daring. Finally he opened both sides and pressed his face against the greased paper.

"I see a dark shape in front of the door!" he exclaimed. "I think it's him. I think he's dead. You must've hit him, Tildie. He's lying right in front of the door."

"Bears don't play possum, do they?" asked Mari from where she sat hugging Evie in their bed.

Tildie lowered the gun. "I don't think so."

Boister ran to the door.

"Wait, Boister. What if he's only stunned?" objected Tildie.

"Then let's get the door open and finish him off before he comes to," answered Boister.

He hauled off the bar and waited for Tildie stand ready, taking aim before he swung the door open.

The bear lay before the door with his nose barely a foot from the opening. His great arms stretched out beside him. The claws looked yellow and vicious even as he lay still.

"I don't think he's breathing," said Boister.

The girls began to whimper.

Boister started to take a step outside.

"Be careful," urged Tildie. "And don't get between the gun and the bear."

Boister nodded and crept toward the huge animal, keeping to the side. He bent over to examine it, and Tildie held her breath, realizing she was praying without having thought out the need.

Suddenly, Boister stood upright, put forth his foot, and carefully nudged the bear. "He's dead," he declared.

The girls cheered, and Tildie staggered backwards to land in the chair by the table. Tears rolled down her cheeks, and the girls came to hug her.

"Why are you crying now?" asked Mari. "Now we're safe."

Boister came over and gave Tildie a pat on the shoulder. "That's just the way women are sometimes," he said sagely to his little sisters. He went back to examine the bear.

"I don't see where you hit him, Tildie." He grabbed the beast by the ears making Tildie shudder and look away.

"The eye, Tildie," he crowed. "You shot him right in the eye."

Tildie looked back, and with the girls help, picked up her crutches to go see for herself.

"That's mighty fine shooting, Tildie," said Boister. "Wait

until Jan hears. That's great. I didn't think you'd ever fired a gun before."

"I haven't, Boister." Tildie gave him a weak smile. "I think we'll have to thank God for my marksmanship. I aimed for his chest."

Boister looked at her, wide-eyed and speechless. He started to grin, then he laughed. Soon, all four of them roared, tears of relief running down their cheeks. They held their aching sides and reveled in the sheer joy of having been delivered from the bear.

When he could talk again, Boister said, "You know what else, Tildie?"

"No, what?" She wiped her apron over her cheeks.

"God also delivered fresh meat and a bearskin rug to our doorstep. If we'd killed this bear someplace else, I couldn't have dragged him home."

Tildie smiled and looked at the bear, trying to see him as a gift left on the doorstep. Suddenly her face brightened. "Boister, I think I remember you can make candles from the tallow off of a bear's fat."

"Hurray!" cried Mari. She grabbed Evie's hands and started bouncing up and down. The two girls did a little dance around the cabin.

Tildie hobbled out to stand next to Boister as he stared admiringly at the bagged bear.

"Tildie?" He tilted his head back to look up at his cousin. "Do you happen to know how to dress a bear?"

Tildie shook her head. "Not one single idea," she admitted.

Boister sighed and looked back down at the huge beast. He put a hand to his head and scratched his scalp with his fingertips. He shrugged and grinned.

"Can't be much more than skinning a deer, and that's just a bit fancier than skinning a rabbit or a squirrel." He put his hand in Tildie's and gave it a squeeze. "We'll manage."

seventeen

Jan would be eternally grateful to the trapper who picked him up, even if the smell which emanated from the old coot was enough to make Jan lose what little was still in his stomach. To be fair, the vomiting might have been due to the crease the bullet had laid across his head. The trapper also gave him a drink from his canteen. That was vastly appreciated. Even if the trapper was not precisely careful with his injuries, he did throw Jan up on the horse and let him ride.

Jan thanked Henderson for not letting him die. The Englishman tended his wounds, dug out the bullet, and declared the bone not broken, only bruised. He fought the fever that threatened to overcome Jan's resolve to live, forced water and broth down him, and prayed over him. He even pulled Jan's Bible out during one of Jan's lucid moments and read to him from Psalms as he was instructed.

Nonetheless, Jan was not grateful for Henderson's interference once he could sit up on the bales of hay serving as his sick bed. "What do you mean I can't go yet?" Jan growled at his nurse. "My family's up there without sufficient provisions. Winter's here. I can't stay down in Fort Reynald with them alone in the cabin."

"Neither can you travel safely," insisted the Englishman. "Your wounds are not sufficiently healed. You haven't regained your strength. The only thing I can say is you've been without fever for all of twenty-four hours. It would be suicide, sir, and what good would you be to your wife and children, dead on the trail?"

Jan threw the tin cup he held across the room.

"And there is the matter of the identity of who ambushed

you," continued Henderson, undaunted by Jan's display of temper. "Your pack horse came back here with its full load. I know, I watched you fasten each item on with my own eyes, and I unloaded those same items with a foreboding in my heart.

"It was because the horse showed up at the fort's gate that I knew you were in trouble. I know you will forgive me for not setting out to search for you, myself, but I have not yet overcome my disability. Therefore, I sent one of the trappers I know to be a good man in my stead."

Jan lowered his head carefully back down to what was serving as his pillow. The Englishman's rhetoric was making the headache worse, if that were possible.

"Your bay is missing, it's true," continued Henderson, ignoring the groan from his patient. "I can't believe someone shot you and left you for dead for one horse and didn't take the one loaded with supplies."

"He just didn't catch Horse," muttered Jan.

"Couldn't catch Horse? Which was the steadier of the two when you stayed with me before? Gert or Horse? Horse! She's the more domesticated of the two. It was Horse who turned around and headed for the nearest stable when she found herself loose."

"Go away, Henderson," groaned Jan. "I bow to your superior judgment for today."

He had to bow to the Englishman's judgment for more than one day. When he did rise from the bed, he swayed. Henderson told him it was loss of blood. His vision blurred. Henderson said it was due to a concussion. His knees buckled. Henderson said it was weakness from the fever. Jan threw a boot at him. Henderson said he was getting better.

❧

Few of the trappers were in the habit of visiting with the stuffy ex-butler. Instead, they congregated around the potbellied stove of the main mercantile building. Most of these men would spend the entire winter in the relative comfort of the fort, gambling, drinking, and occasionally having what they called fandangos where the men got liquored up enough to dance wildly to the Mexican guitars even without female partners. In early spring, those men would disperse into the mountains to trap the furs at their peak of splendor.

Jan and Henderson had plenty of time to talk and, since he was good for little else, Jan began telling stories as he was in the habit of doing with the children. Henderson found them amusing and eventually asked another man to join them. By the end of the second week, Jan entertained a room full of men. It was one form of entertainment available at the fort.

Most mountain men practiced telling tall tales. They enjoyed having someone with stories they hadn't heard before—someone who also appreciated the telling of their outlandish yarns. When Jan began to end the evening storytelling sessions with preaching, they stayed to listen.

Predicted heavy snowfall was a topic of much speculation. Determining whether or not it would be an especially hard winter depended upon woolly worms and how high off the ground the hornets had nested that year. Jan listened to all these conjectures with growing alarm. Although skeptical of the old sayings, he wanted to return to Tildie and the children with all possible speed. One night, he announced to Henderson that he was leaving the next day. In the morning there was two feet of snow on the ground.

"It'll melt quick," advised one of the trappers. "First snow never stays."

Jan was frustrated, but knew the foolishness of starting off in uncertain weather. Two gray cold days followed, spitting snow out of the clouds in frequent flurries. On the third day, a burst of sunshine and a quick thaw surprised the fort. Jan made plans to borrow a riding horse from Henderson and repack Horse. He was determined to set out before yet another spell of bad weather delayed him.

"I don't want you brought back across a saddle, sir," said Henderson.

"Then we won't make it known than I'm leaving, answered Jan. "I'll slip out at first light tomorrow morning."

The only difference in their nightly routine was that when Jan presented the gospel that night to the trappers, he made a more obvious push for the men to make a decision for accepting Christ.

In the morning, he left before most of the fort's populace awoke.

eighteen

Boister and Mari struggled under the weight of the huge skin. They'd cleared a place in the snow where they intended to stretch and peg the hide, hair side down. Scraps of fat and tissue still adhered to the hide, and their next job was to remove them by scraping the inner surface with smooth rocks. But for now, they were having a time of it trying to drag the heavy skin over to the prepared spot.

"Need some help?"

"Jan!" squealed Mari. She dropped her end of the bearskin, and ran through the snow.

"Tildie, Tildie!" yelled Boister, abandoning the skin. "Jan's back."

Evie and Tildie rushed out of the cabin, running to throw their arms around Jan. He kissed them all around, even Boister, then kissed Tildie once more for good measure.

"Oh, Jan," exclaimed Tildie. "You're so thin and pale. What happened?"

"Where's Gert?" asked Boister. Boister looked with disdain upon the borrowed horse and then beyond, to the trees expecting his Gert to come through the thicket.

"Gert's probably running with some Indians' herd by now," explained Jan.

"You lost Gert?" Boister sounded hurt. His face began to crumple. "We lost Gladys, too. She just went off one day and didn't come back. I looked for her, Jan. I tried to follow her tracks, but I lost them in a thick wood."

"She's an old dog, Boister," Jan began.

"She never would've run off," Boister said through a sniffle.

"No, son, you're right," agreed Jan. "She knew a lot about

128

taking care of herself, but sometimes things happen even to those who are good at taking care of themselves. She may be dead, and if she never returns, we have to remember what a happy life she led."

"Let's take Jan inside and have his story," suggested Tildie. "It looks to me like we almost lost him."

They led Jan into the cabin where Tildie'd been slicing thin strips of bear meat to dip in boiling salt water in preparation for drying.

Jan gladly sat and rested while Boister took the horses into the stable and unloaded them.

"Don't you be looking too closely at those bundles, Boister," instructed Jan. "I've got surprises in there that'll have to keep 'til Christmas."

"Presents, Evie," Mari explained.

The little girls' eyes perked up as they turned to carefully watch their brother, hoping something would accidentally fall open. They even rushed to help carry the different bundles when Jan began directing Boister as to where to put them. Tildie sat on Jan's lap, where he'd pulled her when he first sat in the chair by the table.

"Here," Jan said as he shifted her from one side to the other. "Sit facing this way and lean against the other shoulder."

"Why?" asked Tildie, looking closely at his face. She didn't like the lines of pain she saw around his mouth. She tried to get up, but he held her.

"No, Tildie, be still." He firmly gripped her. "I've waited over a month to hold you again, and as long as you don't squirm, I'm okay."

"Jan," she spoke softly. "Tell me what happened."

Before he could begin Boister and Mari launched into the tale of the bear, starting with his marauding around the cabin and stealing their meat.

"I'm glad you're back, Jan," said Boister with a big grin. "Now I don't have to do all the work around here anymore."

"Shame!" exclaimed Tildie in mock indignation, "as if that were the only reason we're glad he's back."

"Stories!" Evie clapped her hands together.

Mari was silent. She came to stand beside Jan and put her little hand on his big arm. "I'm glad you're back 'cause I love you. You don't have to tell stories if you don't want to." Big tears welled up in her eyes. "You don't have to do work. Just, please, never go away again. I missed you."

Jan wrapped his free arm around her little shoulders and kissed her on the top of her head. "I don't ever want to go away again, Mari," he said. "But I can't promise that. I may need to go for supplies. But I want you to know that I missed you, too. I tried my best to get back here as soon as I could."

Evie moved closer and gave Tildie a push as she had often done before. "Tildie, move. Evie's turn."

Tildie relinquished her spot on Jan's lap. As soon as Tildie sat in her chair next to him, Boister surprised her by coming to stand close. He leaned against her leg, moving it aside and then sat on the edge of her chair with her. Mari crawled into Jan's lap to sit with her little sister.

"Now tell us," Mari commanded.

Jan laughed, happy to be with his adopted family. He told of his uneventful trip to the fort, then listed some of the things he had purchased. He left out his unpleasant encounter with des Reaux, but detailed an account of his friendship with Henderson. He told how Henderson feared open spaces and mimicked his English accent making them all laugh as he relayed how often Henderson had served him tea. Then he told how he'd been shot and minimized the painful trip back to the fort and the days of being weak and helpless.

"But all the time I was away from you, I wanted very much to hurry back. And while I was sick, I thought of a plan. It's really an extension of a plan I already had, but I want to put it before you and see if it meets with your approval."

Three little heads bobbed up and down. Tildie tilted hers with a look of inquiry.

"I've asked Tildie to marry me," continued Jan. "That means she'd be my wife and the mother of my children."

Mari clapped her hands. Boister cheered.

"But I feel like you three are already my children. I love you and want us to be a family. If we would agree to be a family, then I'd be your pa and Tildie'd be your mama. We'd live together until you're all grown up and want homes of your own. When I go away on a trip, Mari, you'll know that I'll come back because I'd be your pa, and a pa would do anything possible to get back to his children."

Mari had no second thoughts. She put her arms around Jan's neck, making him wince a bit as she hugged tightly against his sore shoulder.

"Yes," she pronounced enthusiastically. "Can I call you Pa?"

Jan smiled and nodded.

Mari released him and jumped off his lap to climb into Tildie's and hug her. "You can be my mama," she said.

Evie looked at the grown-ups with a puzzled frown between her eyes.

Jan spoke to her carefully, looking into her trusting eyes. "Evie, can I be your pa?"

She still looked unsure as to what was going on. "Pa," she tried the word. Then she looked at Tildie, and a smile grew on her face. "Tildie-ma," she laughed.

That seemed to settle that vote. Jan, Tildie, and Mari turned to look at Boister. He pulled away from Tildie and stood straight, a wary look on his face.

Mari watched him anxiously, then turned with a question for Jan. "Jan," she asked. "Will my real mama and pa be mad because we got a new mama and a new pa?"

"No, Mari," said Jan with confidence. "They'd be happy because families are a good thing, and God likes families."

She turned to Tildie with the same question in her eyes.

"Your mama would be pleased," said Tildie. "She was my very special aunt, and she helped take care of me when I was your age. She taught me how to love children, and she would be happy to know I was taking care of you as your mama."

Mari's face relaxed with relief, and she slid down to go to her brother. Cautiously, she took his hand in her own.

"It's okay, Boister," she spoke quietly. "We don't have to say Mama and Pa unless we want to. But will you please say it's okay? I want to be a family and we can't without you. There's nobody else to be the brother. You *have* to say yes."

Boister didn't jerk away from her or reply quickly with a harsh answer. He looked first at her, then at the others in the room, waiting. He nodded solemnly. "It's okay," he said.

"Hallelujah!" shouted Jan. He plopped Evie on the floor next to her sister and stood. "Let's have a wedding."

Everyone laughed. Mari grabbed her sister's hands and began her own wild version of a polka with her willing partner. Jan pulled Tildie to her feet. He looked down at her with such ardent eyes that Tildie blushed. She ducked her head.

"Jan Borjesson, you said we wouldn't wed until I could stand at the ceremony," she objected with teasing in her voice.

Boister surprised them by answering, "Tildie, you were walking around the cabin without your crutches until the gun knocked you over yesterday. You can't use that as an excuse. The real problem is the cake. You gotta have cake at a wedding."

"How do you know that?" asked Mari.

" 'Cause Mama told me about her cake and the dancing and the party at her wedding."

"It's too late to bake a cake tonight," explained Tildie. "And I don't know how tasty a cake would be without any eggs. We could wait until tomorrow to have the wedding."

"No, we can't." Jan vetoed that idea.

"I could set the dough tonight, and we could have fried bread with sugar coating for breakfast," suggested Tildie.

"Hurray!" cried Mari and Boister together.

"Jan, what am I going to wear?" asked Tildie.

"I brought you a whole bunch of material," he answered.

"Jan, I cannot make a dress in an hour," she objected.

"Don't make a dress out of it," he declared. "Just kinda wrap it around."

"A toga, a toga," squealed Mari happily.

"I'm going to get married in a toga, without a cake or a preacher, with a half-skinned bear on the table."

"Not half-skinned, Tildie," said Boister indignantly. "His whole skin is outside."

"I'll clean up the mess while you wash and fashion some kind of wedding dress," promised Jan. "The girls and Boister will help me, and we'll have bear steak for dinner. I'll cook."

"You really want to get married tonight, don't you?" she asked.

He looked in her eyes and nodded slowly. She blushed.

"All right," she said in a voice of resignation. "If this family is going to insist, I guess my only choice is to comply." She stole a look at Jan, who was still watching her, and blushed again. "Where's the material for my wedding dress, Jan Borjesson?"

nineteen

As a religious ceremony of proper decorum and solemnity, the wedding failed completely. As a joyous celebration, it excelled everyone's expectations.

Of the three pieces of material, Tildie chose the golden calico over the red or the more somber blue. She suddenly insisted that she wash her hair, and the bath took longer than pleased Jan. He and Boister finished what they could of the bear meat and cleaned up the remnants of that messy business. Then the little girls giggled as Jan took a bath in the stable with Boister carrying the pots of warm water to him.

The sun set before they stood together in front of the fireplace. Jan read words from his Bible, and they exchanged their vows quietly, looking into each other's faces and perfectly content with what they saw there. The silver ring was just a little loose, but Tildie and the children exclaimed over its beauty.

Afterwards, they danced to Jan's loud renditions of old Swedish folk songs. Tildie sang several of the songs she'd learned from her father. The children sang along when they knew the words. Mari insisted that they sing the sums song which they'd made up to learn their addition facts. Finally, they sat down to the wedding feast which included pieces of hard candy Jan had brought up from the fort.

The over-excited children resisted going to their beds. Jan insisted they go. In his rich baritone, Jan sang a lullaby his grandmother and mother had sung to him while Tildie sat on his lap in the deerskin-covered chair. When the children were still restless, he and Tildie harmonized melodious hymns. Finally, the children finished their squirming and slept. The newlyweds watched the flickering light of the fireplace.

"Our voices sound good together," commented Jan.

"Uh-huh," Tildie responded dreamily.

"Are you tired?"

"I haven't slept well while you were gone—especially since the bear started worrying us. Since we shot him. . .my goodness was that only yesterday? It's been a busy two days."

"Are you happy?"

"Yes," said Tildie. "It wasn't the wedding I dreamed of, but it sure is chock full of good memories."

He ran a finger down the edge of the material that formed the neckline of her toga. "I thought my bride was beautiful. Your gown is beautiful." He buried his face in her hair. "Your hair is beautiful. Your eyes are beautiful. Your smile is. . ."

"I know," said Tildie, "beautiful."

"No," said Jan. "I mean, it's beautiful, but I thought of another word. Your smile is charming."

Tildie giggled and rested her head against his uninjured shoulder. "You look tired, Jan."

"I am," he admitted. "Henderson said I was foolish to travel, but he didn't know what was waiting for me here." He kissed her.

"Jan, when we get back to a settlement with a preacher, would you mind if we got married again?"

"You don't feel married."

"I don't know," admitted Tildie. "It's so different from what I imagined." Another giggle escaped her. "You know, I actually think our wedding was better."

Jan nuzzled her neck and she squirmed. "That tickles," she objected.

"Tildie, I'd like to pick you up and carry you to our bed, but I don't think I can."

"Are you too tired?" she asked with real concern. She had gotten a glimpse over the half wall of the ugly red scar high on his chest when he'd stood up in the stable. She touched the scar on his forehead where the bullet had just missed ending his life.

"I admit my shoulder is aching something fierce, but I'm not too tired to love you."

She didn't speak.

"What about you, Tildie?" he asked softly. "Are you recovered enough to be my wife?"

She tensed, her back straightening as she unconsciously pulled away from his embrace. She took a deep breath and made herself relax. Purposefully she nestled down in his arms. "I'm a little nervous."

He put his lips against her ear. "So am I," he whispered.

"Let's go to bed," she suggested and stood. He came up right after her and wrapped her in his arms. After kissing her one more time, he lost the nervousness. Now, she smiled at him with no shyness at all, and they walked over to the little niche that contained the pine needle mattress. Jan had hung a blanket across the opening to give Tildie the privacy she needed for her bath. He pushed an edge aside and led his bride through.

≈

"Get up, get up." An insistent voice roused the sleeping adults. "You promised to make fried bread."

Tildie opened her eyes to find Mari and Evie standing on one side of the bed and Boister on the other. She blushed at the three pairs of eyes staring at her intently and burrowed down further in the covers.

Jan sat up and looked groggily at the invaders.

"Rule Number One for the Borjesson family: The mother and father are to be left alone in their bed until they wake up. You children get on the other side of that blanket."

His voice of authority sent them scurrying around the edge of the blanket.

"Now," said Jan. "One of you call to wake us up. We're now asleep again." He laid back down and took Tildie in his arms.

There was some giggling and whispered consultation from the other side. Mari's voice piped up. "Mama, Pa, can we have breakfast now?"

Jan turned a grinning face to Tildie's. "Yes, daughter," he answered. "Put some wood on the fire, and I'll be out as soon as I'm dressed."

"We already put the wood on," said Boister. "We've been waiting an awful long time."

"Mama?" Evie's voice sounded plaintive.

"I'll be out in a minute, Evie," answered Tildie past the lump in her throat. "Sit in Mama's chair and wait patiently."

Jan leaned over to kiss her as he got out of bed.

"No need to hurry, Honey. I'll take care of them."

"She called me mama," Tildie whispered.

"Well, don't cry about it," he admonished her with a laugh. "Pretty soon they'll be mama-ing you to death."

Tildie smiled at the prospect.

While Jan and Boister took care of the chores, Tildie, Evie, and Mari made the fried bread. First, they took out a starter from their crock of sourdough to set aside for the next batch of dough. Then the girls pinched off dime-sized pieces, and Tildie dropped them into a deep kettle of smoking-hot fat. When the pieces rose to the surface, Tildie turned them with a long, forked stick. When they glistened golden brown on all sides and smelled heavenly, she lifted them out, and the girls waited until they drained and cooled a bit before rolling them in sugar. The little puffs of sweet dough were a treat. They'd not had enough sugar to lavish on these delicacies for quite a while.

There was plenty of work to do that first morning. The bear meat and skin must be taken care of without delay. With Jan to help, the whole procedure took less time. Soon the skin was staked and scraped. The meat hung in strips in a smoke house, and they put big hunks away in the cave. Jan and Boister worked to make the storage cave more secure.

"Black bears don't hibernate as the grizzly does," explained Jan. "They sleep most of the winter away, but they can wake up two or three times or maybe more and wander away from their den. This one just didn't see any reason to settle down when he had such interesting folk to investigate every night. Perhaps later in the winter he would have settled in for longer naps.

"This bear will make our winter more luxurious," he continued. "Why, we'll have grease to waterproof our boots and use on our hands when they get chapped by the cold, dry air. It makes a good throat rub and hair oil. Mighty good thing Tildie shot this bear." Jan grinned at Boister. They both knew it was only the hand of God that directed the bullet to the right place. Tildie really didn't deserve much credit when it came to slaying the beast. She'd been brave to stand before the charging bear, but it was a blessing her shot hit the target.

Inside, Tildie and the girls rendered the fat in preparation for making candles. They'd save some of the fat for cooking and making soap. Tildie encouraged the girls to be speedy with their chores.

"As soon as we're finished with this old bear, I can make you some dresses," she explained.

The girls wanted new dresses, so they swept and washed dishes. Even little Evie helped as best she could with all the little chores that would have kept Tildie away from her hot kettle. Their new mama guarded the boiling grease and wouldn't let them near.

The days that followed brought the new family closer together. Through the cold November, they played games, heard stories, sang songs, and did lessons with both Tildie and Jan. Jan began teaching Boister to shoot his rifle, but held off telling the boy that the gun was his until Christmas. Tildie sewed new dresses and shirts. The material which had been her wedding gown made a beautiful dress and her favorite to wear. She made shirts for both Jan and Boister out of the more somber blue, and the little girls had three dresses apiece plus new petticoats and aprons.

For a Christmas surprise, she stitched matching dresses out of the scraps for the little girls' dolls, and hemmed handkerchiefs for the whole family. Boister and Jan worked on a secret in the stable. It was easy to tell that their project involved wood, but the ladies of the household refrained from snooping.

The isolated family had no idea what the date was on the calendar, so when the projects were near completion, Jan announced that Christmas would be celebrated in exactly seven days. That sent the little cabin's occupants into a flurry of last minute preparations including decorating, baking, and finishing their gifts.

"Why didn't you just say that tomorrow would be Christmas?" asked Tildie.

"What, Tildie?" he exclaimed. "Were you never a child? Part of the fun of Christmas is waiting and it seeming like it'll never come."

Their Christmas morning was simple, but filled with the kind of things that make memories sweet. Even Evie, with Jan's help, had made a trivet for Tildie so she could put the hot kettle on the table. Jan's gifts from the fort were exclaimed over. They donned the clothes quickly and paraded before the others. Jan told story after story, some from the Bible, and some which were sentimental Christmas happenings from his own past.

In the evening after all the gaiety had wound down and there was a cozy atmosphere in the cabin, Boister read the Christmas story from Luke with some help from Jan. He'd been practicing all week, but he still tripped over some words.

"A very satisfying Christmas," Jan murmured to Tildie that night as they lay in bed. "Last year, I was all alone except for Gladys. Somehow, having a family to share the celebration with makes the whole thing more beautiful."

"I suppose that's because God's intention in having His Son come to earth was to share the Good News with all people."

"A lonely vigil is just not in keeping with the spirit of Christmas," agreed Jan.

"When you think that the shepherds shouted for joy, and the skies filled with angels praising His Name. . . ."

"It just seems impossible to make it a sober, quiet occasion, doesn't it?"

"Yes, impossible," agreed Tildie.

twenty

In February, Tildie was sure that there would be an additional member of their family. A few mornings of nausea confirmed her suspicions, and Jan seemed pleased with the news.

"Remember a long time ago when you asked if my babies would be your sisters, Mari?" Tildie introduced the subject one morning as they did lessons.

Mari frowned for a minute in contemplation, then smiled as she recalled. "You said they'll be my cousins."

"Yes, I said that then, but now—because we've decided to be a family with Jan—it's different. Next fall, you'll have a baby brother or a baby sister."

"You're going to have a baby?" asked Boister.

Tildie smiled at them all. "Yes."

Boister looked at Jan and grinned. "I hope it's a boy, Pa. We're already outnumbered."

Jan looked astonished. In the three months since the wedding, Boister had always avoided calling Jan anything. When he had to relay a message to someone in the house he would say, *your Pa* wants you, or *he* says to. . . Now Jan had finally been called Pa and he wanted to shout with joy. Instead he grinned back at Boister and said, "Yep, but if God gives us another girl to take care of, we'll just have to figure it's because we've been doing such a good job with the ones we've already got."

Jan did take good care of his new family. Tildie had mostly recovered from her accident. She still limped noticeably but only occasionally became over-tired and ached in her bones. She joked that she would be one of those people who would be able to predict a spell of bad weather by the pain in her legs. Tildie felt confident that God had ordained this marriage, that her life was just as it should be, and God was pleased.

࿇

Tildie and Jan sat out in the yard of their cabin, enjoying the cool night air and watching for shooting stars. They sat on a blanket on the ground with their backs against a pile of logs. With Jan's arm around her, Tildie felt comfortable and secure.

"As I see it, Mrs. Borjesson," said Jan, "we have numerous options as to where to live and raise our family."

Tildie tilted up her head where it rested on his shoulder so she could see his face.

"Pray tell," she grinned.

"We can live here, go back and live with the Arapaho, take over the children's ranch, or go back to Ohio where my family would welcome you with open arms."

"Which do you prefer?" she asked, trying not to be anxious. She had her own desires but realized she'd never be happy if Jan went where she preferred and then wasn't happy, himself.

"I'm a little tired of wilderness living to tell the truth," Jan explained. "I'd like to settle where there are some other people."

Tildie held her breath. The Arapaho Indians were "other people," and as much as she'd grown to like and respect Older One, she did not regard living the nomadic and difficult life of the Indians as a pleasant future. Still, if God had called Jan to be a missionary to the Indians, she must comply.

She slowly let out the breath she had been holding. As the air left her lungs, she tried to mentally let go of her will to dictate the future.

"The passion I had to tell the Indians of our Lord," continued her husband, "seems to have transferred to another area of service."

"What's that, Jan?"

"Part of it's raising the children," he said seriously. "I haven't completely come to understand, but it seems to revolve around preparing the next generation of Christians. I feel the need to be a part of a community, to preach regularly, to be in a church every week."

Tildie merely nodded, not wanting to interrupt his thoughts as he strove to share them with her.

"The ranch is waiting for the children to return, and you said there was a settlement close by. I think I would like to go to the children's ranch, keep it going so Boister would have that as his heritage from his parents, and serve as pastor in that community. Do they have a church?"

"No," admitted Tildie. The homestead held no fond memories for her. The little prairie house had been a home of unhappiness. She wasn't sure this was the best plan, but she held her peace. Jan would change the atmosphere of the run-down ranch. Under his guidance, it would again prosper and be a new place, different from what it had been. She had confidence in Jan.

It wasn't until the next day while she was busy with some mundane chore that the little voice of doubt crept in. John Masters had married her aunt merely to have possession of a prime piece of land, but that had nothing to do with Jan.

As more of the snow thawed, Jan took Boister out a couple of times each week to check the passes they'd need to traverse to get down out of the mountains. The woolly worms had been right and the footage of snow collected in shaded spots was remarkable. In April, Jan finally announced they would be leaving as soon as Tildie said they were packed up.

"No need to take everything, Tildie," Jan informed her. "We'll leave the cabin so that if somebody stumbles on to it, they can use it. Dishes and blankets can all be replaced easier than we can tote them with us. Leave whatever staples that will keep, too. It might save somebody's life." They also left wood cut and stacked, candles, and a flint box, some heavy pans, and of course, all the furniture.

"The ranch has all we'll need," said Jan and left the cabin to see about the meat in the cave which would not keep.

"How does he know the ranch has all we need?" Tildie asked herself.

"Mama, Mama," Mari's voice called urgently from far away. Tildie dropped the blanket she'd folded and ran to the door, her heart in her throat. The last time a child had called like that, a bear had been right at his heels.

She stood in the doorway of the cabin and looked directly at the place Boister had broken through the brush on the run. Sure enough, Mari stumbled out of the woods in almost exactly the same spot, but she wasn't running, and she held a golden, furry bundle in her arms. Tildie took several steps out of the cabin.

Following Mari, several clumsy pups bounced through the short weeds. The last out of the thicket was Gladys. Gladys! Tildie began to run in her awkward gait. Out of the corner of her eye, she saw Jan and Boister descending the hill from the cave, hurrying to meet the lost dog.

Gladys barked joyously and ran from one member to the next, licking faces. When the greetings subsided, Tildie asked, "Mari, where did you find her?"

"She found me!" exclaimed the happy child. "Look, she has puppies." She did, indeed. Puppies surrounded Jan as if they recognized their mother's master.

"Five," shouted Boister. "Five puppies!"

Jan roughed the fur around Gladys's neck. "Well, old girl, who'd have thought you'd be a mother again at this late date? Let's look at these puppies and see if we can distinguish what kind of dog you've been friendly with."

He sat down on the grass amidst the dogs and kids. Evie promptly plopped in his lap, and Boister captured a puppy for him to inspect.

Jan examined the fluffy fur, rounded ears, squarish muzzle, and short body. "I don't see any wolf in these pups," he announced.

"Where did she find a father for them, then?" asked Tildie.

"Remember the Indians keep dogs."

Tildie did remember that the Arapaho kept dogs for eating, among other things. The thought had bothered her.

"Are there Indians close by?" asked Tildie who had thought they were rather remote from any other humans.

"Some," said Jan, vaguely. "There's a winter camp near Manitou Springs. That's pretty far for Gladys to have gone visiting. Well, if she spoke English, she might tell us, but we'll probably never know."

He rose from the ground easily and hoisted Evie up to his shoulder. "I suppose you want to take the dogs with us on our journey."

Tildie gasped. How could he even think of leaving them behind?

The children began to clamor their insistence, and Tildie looked at Jan closely. A twinkle in his eye as he looked down at the mass of kids and dogs at his feet gave him away. He intended all along to take the pups. He was enjoying Boister's and Mari's claims that the dogs would be no trouble, that they would each personally take care of them, and make sure the pups weren't in the way.

At last Jan took pity on them and gracefully acquiesced to their request. Gladys and her brood would travel with them.

In the morning they set out. Evie and the pups rode on the travois when they were tired. Mari preferred to ride on Charlie. Boister walked more than he had on their previous trip, and Tildie was struck with how mature he was becoming. *He's almost seven*, she thought. Yet, he marched alongside Jan as if he were twice that age. Tildie walked some too, but her back and legs began to ache and Jan insisted she ride, so she stretched out on the travois.

"This isn't much better," she complained as Evie nestled down beside her and the pups tried to lick her face. Jan just laughed.

Tildie was surprised to learn they were going to Fort Reynald.

"Why?" she asked. She had no desire to meet the Frenchman who could have become her husband.

"I want to check on Henderson," replied Jan. "You'll enjoy meeting him. Remember, he saved my life. You might think of something you need before we start out across the prairie. Also, it's a good idea to check on the mood of the Indians before we cross their territory."

"You mean they might be hostile?"

"Probably not," said Jan. "Or at least, no more than usual. But they have feuds between the tribes, and it's smart to know where the disputes are festering."

Tildie closed her eyes in prayer. She just wanted to get home, wherever that might be. She hoped it was someplace where they wouldn't be constantly afraid of wild things— whether they were bears or renegades.

twenty-one

Tildie entered the gates of Fort Reynald with trepidation. They immediately went to the livery. There, the genuine friendliness of Henderson, combined with his interesting accent, did much to alleviate her uneasiness. It was decided that they would accept his humble hospitality for the evening meal and camp outside the walls of the fort with many other visitors.

About thirty tepees gathered around the decrepit wooden structure passing for a fort. Some were occupied by Arapaho, some by Cheyenne, and several by trappers. An uneasy peace reigned between the Indians and trappers. The natives tolerated the traders because they obliged them in their own passion to dicker and barter. Most Indians looked down upon the trappers as interlopers.

When Henderson offered them tea, Jan, standing behind the Englishman, smiled at Tildie with an I-told-you-so look in his eye. The children enjoyed taking tea with the man who spoke so oddly. They giggled because he sounded just as Jan had imitated, and Boister went so far as to say that a "cup of tea would be most welcome." His imitation of Jan's imitation of Henderson's accent made them all laugh. Henderson knew he was being made sport of and took it good-naturedly.

"I have a request of you, my giant friend," he said when the children finished their tea and scooted outside.

"What is it?" asked Jan. "You know I'm willing to oblige if it's within my ability."

"I want to go back East."

"Cross the prairie?" Jan could not hide the incredulous tone which invaded his voice.

"I think I can do it in your company and with the strength of Jesus."

"You're welcome to come with us, but we plan to travel only as far as the North Fork of the Cimarron in western Kansas territory. Why do you want to leave?"

"Rumor has it that the new inspector for Indian affairs will be more thorough this summer. None of the traders at this fort have a license, and with the unscrupulous competition of the Bent brothers, business is failing anyway. Most of the Indians have gone to trade either south, at Fort El Pueblo; or east, at Bent's Fort. Fort Reynald will surely fold before the end of the summer and then I would be stuck here with my own company. I'd rather try to make my way east with you."

Jan looked over at Tildie who nodded her head slightly, indicating she had no objection.

"Fine, Henderson," said Jan, "you're welcome to join us."

"I feel compelled to issue a warning," Henderson continued.

"What about?"

"Des Reaux is in a black mood. He took a Mexican woman to wife this winter, and she grew tired of him quickly. She left him with a knife wound in his side when she departed at the first opportunity.

"He's not pleased at being forced out of business by the Bents. Then, too, several traders drank a bit too much one evening just last week and decided to display their dislike of the Frenchman before they left for the summer. They tied him up and trashed his side of the mercantile building, leaving the other side in fairly decent order. In short, des Reaux is spoiling for a fight."

"We'll stay out of his way," commented Jan.

Henderson nodded.

"I do have something you might consider valuable for our journey," offered Henderson.

Jan merely lifted his eyebrows in inquiry.

"I had a small wagon given to me in lieu of payment.

"Humph!" she looked away, embarrassed. "You're beautiful wife has a red nose, puffy eyes, and a swollen body."

Jan grinned and nodded. "Looks great to me."

Tildie turned back to him, and a smile broke through her tears. Jan had a way of banishing all her doubts. She could believe he honestly loved her when he sat beside her and looked at her with that warmth in his eyes.

Many of the men at the fort smelled from the lack of personal hygiene, but a rancid odor suddenly invaded the quiet talk between Jan and his wife and wrenched them out of their self-absorption.

Jan stood as soon as the shadow touched him. "Des Reaux," he acknowledged the man's presence.

"Borjesson." The Frenchman nodded, seemingly undaunted by the fact that Jan towered over him. He worked the toothpick from one corner of his mouth to the other while staring boldly at Tildie. "This is your wife?"

"Tildie," Jan spoke as he put a hand on her arm and drew her to stand beside him. He put a protective arm around her shoulders. "This is Armand des Reaux, the grocer at Fort Reynald."

Tildie knew she must remain calm. She fought the feeling of disgust which rose in her throat as she assessed the repellent nature of the man before her. This was the man John Masters had expected her to marry? This repulsive, malodorous, vulgar pig was his idea of a husband for her? She now realized how truly John Masters must have despised her.

She nodded, acknowledging the introduction but unable to voice any suitable pleasantries.

The Frenchman's eyes narrowed, and he insolently looked her over.

"Amazing, Borjesson," he spoke with false congeniality. "Your wife looks so young to be the mother of three children."

Jan's grip on her shoulders tightened.

"I take good care of her, des Reaux."

The coldness in her husband's voice sent a shiver down her spine. Surely, the Frenchman would get the message. Jan stood between her and des Reaux. A flood of gratitude filled her as she realized that God had given her a giant Swede to protect her from this unsavory person.

"Welcome to the fort, my little friend." The congenial tone of des Reaux's words still contained an underlying threat. "The sunshine of your presence is long overdue in this godforsaken hole. An entire year overdue, *mon cherie*."

Tildie felt the rigidity intensify in her husband's stance. The last thing she wanted to see was a fight between these two men. Jan was undoubtedly the stronger of the two, but the Frenchman impressed her as the type to use a knife instead of settling their disagreement with just their fists. She found the courage to speak.

"Thank you for your welcome, Mr. des Reaux." She smiled up at Jan's face, ignoring the rigid set of his jaw and the thin line of his lips. Determinedly, she went on. "I'm happy to be with my husband here in Colorado. I, too, thought this area might be godforsaken, until Jan reminded me of God's goodness."

She turned innocent eyes upon the antagonistic Frenchman. "Perhaps you don't know the promise God gives His children. In the Bible it says He will never leave us nor forsake us, no matter what the circumstances. I lost sight of that while waiting in the Indian camp."

"Spoken like a true wife of a preacher," conceded the Frenchman. His eyes lost none of the hard glitter which chilled her heart. He removed the crude toothpick from his mouth and grinned widely, showing his yellowed teeth.

In an effort to find something legitimate to focus on other than this despicable man, Tildie shifted her gaze to the children. They stood in a line behind the man, having abandoned their game. The solemn faces of the Indian children told their hatred for the Frenchman. Their narrowed eyes bored holes in the back of the grocer. They watched his every move intently, showing their distrust. Boister had taken Mari's hand. Mari held Evie's.

Do they remember? wondered Tildie. *Do they realize this is the man their stepfather intended me to marry?* Boister's stony expression could mean he remembered or just recognized this Frenchman as the same type of evil man as John Masters.

"Mama," whimpered Evie.

Tildie held out her hand. "Come, Evelyn. Let's go see about fixing dinner."

Evie ran to grab her hand.

"Good day, Mr. des Reaux." Tildie turned a disinterested shoulder on the Frenchman and marched away with a straight back and head held high.

"A truly magnificent woman." Des Reaux watched her as she departed. Suddenly, a large hand grabbed the shirt front below the man's leering face, lifting him off the ground.

"Be careful how you look at my wife, des Reaux." Jan's voice was a low growl. "My God orders men to treat their wives as He treats His church. I understand that to mean I should be willing to die for my family. *This* preacher knows how to fight."

Des Reaux made a deprecating movement with his hands and gasped out a disclaimer as best he could. "I have no interest in your wife."

The Swede dropped des Reaux, and he collapsed in the dirt. Jan clenched his fists at his side determined not to pound the little weasel into the ground.

"Come, children," he ordered and turned on his heel, leaving the angry Frenchman muttering in the dust.

twenty-two

"We can leave tomorrow." Jan held a supply list the three adults and three children had labored over the night before. They sat at Henderson's table, but Tildie and Mari had made the breakfast. Now, as Jan reached for the last of Tildie's tasty biscuits, he told Boister to put a skip in his step and get ready to go to the mercantile.

"I want to go," begged Mari. "Please."

"No," said Jan as he pushed the last bite in his mouth and wiped his hands on his pant legs. "The men in the fort don't have the manners I'd expect to be shown before my daughters." He took a mug from Henderson's table and lifted it to his lips. With his head tipped back, he drained it and set it back down with a thud. He then rubbed his forearm across his mouth wiping away any wetness.

The sight of the expression on Tildie's face arrested the movement in mid-swipe. One of her finely drawn eyebrows arched in mock indignation, and a smile quivered at the corner of her mouth.

"What?" he asked.

"The trappers have no manners?" She looked pointedly at the arm that still rested against his mouth.

At that moment, Henderson came in from the other room. "Would you care for more tea, Madame?" he asked, holding the tin pot he used for brewing with the same elegance he would have held a teapot of Wedgewood china.

Jan dropped both arms to his sides and looked from the former butler to his wife. "Tildie, you're not comparing me to Henderson here."

The look of absolute horror on his face brought laughter

bubbling out of Tildie. She laughed until her side hurt and tears ran down her face. Long before she could recover, Jan shot her a disgusted look, waved at Boister to "come on," and left to buy the supplies they would need on the trail.

❧

"That's about all we can do to make it comfortable," Jan said as he moved a barrel to the side and began strapping it to the wooden arch that held the canvas over the wagon bed. "With those boxes padded with buffalo robes and blankets, it should make a fairly comfortable bed."

Tildie stood on tiptoe with her hands on the back of the wagon, trying to see in. Jan turned her towards him and lifted, holding her snug against his chest.

"Can you see better now?" He laughed at her prim expression as she looked around quickly to see who might be watching.

"I see fine," she sputtered.

"You haven't even looked in the wagon," he pointed out.

"Jan, put me down." She struggled weakly.

He kissed her cheek as she turned her face back and forth, still trying to see if anyone was watching them.

"How 'bout I put you down in the wagon and you can stretch out on that makeshift bed to see how it feels?"

"Why?" She quit struggling to admire the fine lines at the corners of his eyes that crinkled so attractively when he smiled at her.

"Henderson and I will be finishing up loading the donkey cart. You need your afternoon nap, and if you're in the wagon, you'll be out of our way as we move around the livery."

"Who will watch the children?"

"Henderson and I can watch the children, and when Evie gets cranky, I'll bring her to the wagon and tell her to take a nap with Mama." He gave her a hug, kissed her lightly on the lips, and swung her up and over the back of the wagon.

"I'll be easier in my mind if you're close to where Henderson and I are working instead of on the outside of the fort where we've been camping."

"Are you worried about des Reaux?"

"I've been praying for protection, but that doesn't mean I'm going to be careless with what God has entrusted to me."

"You're worried about that man?"

Jan looked seriously into her eyes. "Honey, we must be as harmless as doves and as wise as serpents. I believe Armand des Reaux to be evil." He leaned forward and kissed her again. "You take a nap. Tomorrow, we'll be on the trail, and we needn't worry about the Frenchman again."

❧

An hour later, Jan lifted Evie over the tailgate of the wagon. He put a finger to his lips and pointed to Tildie.

"Shh! Little Girl," he cautioned, "crawl in next to your mama and try not to wake her. Take a nice nap, and when both my pretty girls get up, we'll fix supper. Tonight, we'll get to hear Pennsylvania Paterson play his fiddle."

Evie leaned out of the wagon and gave her pa a squeezing hug and a big kiss on the cheek before she turned and crawled over the barrels, boxes, and gunny sacks to where Tildie lay napping. She pulled herself onto the buffalo robes and turned to wave good-bye. She blew another kiss, put her finger to her little lips and hissed a loud "Sh," giggled, and snuggled down. Jan shook his head, grinning at her antics, and returned to the work in the barn. They'd discovered weak boards in the bottom of the cart, and those had to be repaired before they could finish loading it.

"Fire!" The shout was followed by more bellows and the sounds of men running. Henderson and Jan dropped what they were doing and raced out of the livery, into the open square around which the buildings of the fort were built.

The smell of smoke and the sound of the flames crackling as they consumed canvas assaulted the men.

"The wagon," Henderson exclaimed.

Two burly mountain men slashed at the canvas on the Borjesson wagon, ripped it from the frame, and threw it to the ground. Two other men stood beside the wooden wagon and beat the flames with horse blankets. Another man ran up with a bucket of water and emptied it on the flames. He immediately ran back from where he'd come.

"Tildie, Evie!" Jan ran to the end of the wagon and tried to look inside. Heavy smoke choked him and stung his eyes. He could see nothing even as the men pulled off the canvas covering. "Tildie," he shouted again and started to climb in.

Two hands grabbed him from behind. "I'm here. I'm here."

Jan twirled around and grabbed her into a strong embrace. "Evie?" he gasped.

"She's here, too."

He felt the child wrapped around one of his legs before he looked down and saw her. He let Tildie go in order to bend over and peel the frightened child from his leg. He hoisted her into his arms to hold her tightly and pat her back, murmuring words of comfort. He moved them away from the wagon. "I just left her with you."

Tildie smiled through her tears and nodded. "Yes," she agreed, "but you forgot little girls should go potty before they go down for their naps. She woke me and we left the wagon."

Jan looked down at his wife. "Thank God, Tildie!"

She nodded and leaned against him.

The noise around the wagon subsided, and they looked to see the men had put out the fire. They had acted quickly. A fire in the fort of dried wooden structures was a serious threat.

Several of the men came over to where the family had gathered. Boister stood with Mari. Henderson stood behind them with a hand on each of their shoulders.

"Thanks," said Jan to the crowd.

The men signaled their acknowledgement with curt nods. "You okay?" one of them asked Tildie.

"Yes, thank you."

"Did you see the dirt was on fire underneath the wagon?" asked a tall, dark man. He'd been beating the flames.

"What does that mean?" asked another. "Dirt don't burn."

"Kerosene." The man spat in the dirt. "Someone poured it on the canvas, and it dripped on the dirt. You can smell it, too."

"It was des Reaux," said the man who had carried the bucket. "I saw him walking fast toward his place with something under his coat just before I saw the fire."

An angry murmur ran through the group of men. Nobody liked the Frenchman. A fire endangered all of them. Jan sensed that at any moment the men would decide justice was needed, and they were the ones to administer it.

He held up a hand, stopping them just as they were about to turn *en masse* and storm through the fort to the Frenchman's store. "Wait!" he ordered. "First of all, we only *think* he did this. Did anyone see him pour the kerosene? Light the wagon?"

"The swine did it," proclaimed one of the men loudly. "None of us did it, so it must've been him."

"No one else had a reason," agreed another.

"Fine," said Jan. "We'll go talk to him about it. Did you hear what I said? We will *talk* to him."

Jan handed Evie into Tildie's arms and pushed her toward Henderson. "Stay here," he advised and put himself at the front of the band of men marching to the mercantile.

There were seven men behind Jan, and he prayed that he would be able to control the situation. Wrath thrummed through his veins like a tympani. Still the Holy Spirit dampened his anger. This devil had almost hurt Tildie and Evie, but he had no desire to see the Frenchman dangling from a rope, pierced with knives, or whatever else these rough men could think of as "just punishment."

They entered the store, bursting through the wooden door with such force it slammed back against the wall.

Des Reaux dangled from the grip of two mountain men

who had evidently followed him without waiting to discuss the matter. The short man's face was bloodied.

Jan stopped, as did the others behind him. With one look at what had already transpired, the men surged forward, eager to finish the job.

"Stop!" yelled Jan. "I don't want to be as low as this worm."

The other men turned to look at him. This strange statement arrested their attention. Relieved, Jan saw confusion on their faces. He needed to make them think before they plowed ahead, running purely on mindless revenge.

"He's a weasel, an unscrupulous beast," said the preaching Swede. "He's not a human. He's an animal." The two men holding the limp Frenchman aloft lowered him to the floor, but didn't let him go.

Jan took a few steps forward so he could snarl into des Reaux's face. He saw the terror in his eyes and knew the man recognized these mountain men wanted to kill him.

"This is a snake." Jan hissed the words in the frightened man's dirty face. "Like the serpent in the Garden of Eden, he crawls on his belly and brings destruction. This is not a man, but a creature of evil."

Jan turned suddenly to look his listeners in the eye. His steady gaze went from one man to the next. "We recognize him for what he is, because we're not the low, cowardly brute that he is. No man here would douse a man's property with kerosene and torch it. Maybe he thought my wife was in there, or maybe he saw her leave and only wanted to destroy what belonged to me. Either way, his evil jeopardized this entire encampment."

The men grunted agreement and pressed forward. Jan again held up his hand. "But," he exclaimed, "I don't wish to be identified with this scum. I won't join him in his wickedness. I stand apart."

"We'll take care of him for you," volunteered one of the men.

"You don't have to take care of him for me. 'Vengeance is mine, sayeth the Lord.' God Almighty will deal with this man. I pity him. We might hang him, and that few moments of agony would be all that des Reaux had to pay for his crime—but God tells us that for men like des Reaux, He has a lake of fire, a place of never-ending torment. God says He'll throw this man into the outer darkness where there shall be wailing and gnashing of teeth, agony we cannot understand. Do you see why I don't want to be like him?" Jan stopped to gauge how his audience responded. He didn't often rail on about hell and damnation, but he was a preacher, and he knew how to get his point across.

Three hours later, at Tildie's insistence, Henderson went over to see what was happening. He returned to say that it appeared her husband was conducting a revival.

"Can I go listen, Mama?" asked Boister.

Tildie looked at him with a blank expression. She couldn't quite comprehend what had happened. Jan had left with a small mob of men bent on violence. Now he was preaching! Reserved Boister had called her, "Mama," as if it were the most natural thing in the world, and he was hopping from one foot to the other waiting for her to give him permission to go listen to a sermon. She turned questioning eyes to Henderson.

"It would be all right, Madame, if the young man were to sit on the edge of the crowd."

"Crowd?" she whispered.

Henderson smiled. "Jan is standing on the roof of the mercantile, and most of the people in the fort and from the surrounding encampment are gathered in the square. He moved out of the building some time ago when it became too crowded. He must have realized there were people outside who could not hear."

Tildie walked over to the barn door and pushed it open. She saw the backs of people who pressed closer to be able to see and hear her husband. She heard the familiar cadence of his speech but couldn't make out the words.

"Please, Mama," Boister begged.

"I'll watch after the boy," offered Henderson.

"Yes, go," she answered. Boister and Henderson bolted out the door.

"What's Pa doing?" asked Mari.

"He's telling the people about God."

"Like he tells us?"

"Yes," answered Tildie.

"Uh-uh," disagreed Evie from where she stood in the door at Tildie's feet.

Tildie swung her up in her arms. "What do you mean 'uh-uh,' Little One?"

Evie giggled and covered her ears. "Pa yelling!" she exclaimed.

twenty-three

"Well," said Tildie when Jan crawled in beside her, "What happened?"

Jan chuckled. "You know when I headed across that square towards the mercantile, I never expected that I was going to see God working. I thought I had a pretty fair chance of seeing some miserable men claim justice their own way. I was praying mighty hard with every step."

Jan stroked her arm absentmindedly. He sighed with contentment. "It's always a pleasure to watch the Master at work, to see Him turn things around, working all things together for good. To see His way plow through a situation gone sour and turn it up sweet.

"Over thirty—I lost count—of those rough men accepted Christ as their Savior. Seven of the Arapaho decided the same. I tried to keep count so I'd know how many Bibles to send here."

"What about des Reaux?"

"He had the smell of kerosene on the inside of his jacket. Made a perfect example of how sin clings to you and there's nothing you can do to remove the stain, get rid of the smell. Next step was to introduce them to Jesus who washes all their sins away."

"So what's going to happen to des Reaux?" asked Tildie impatiently.

"He's going to be escorted to Bent's Fort, where the U.S. Calvary will take him in hand." Like Fort Reynald, Bent's Fort was actually a privately owned establishment, not a military outpost. It, however, was on the Santa Fe trail, and the U.S. Calvary found its location convenient.

"What about us?" asked Tildie.

"Well, I don't think we'll be leaving tomorrow, but we should be heading out by the middle of next week. Des Reaux generously donated any supplies we lost in the fire out of his stock."

"He did?"

"Well, I think he thought that would barter him out of his predicament."

Tildie thought this over and decided she wouldn't inquire as to how that came about. She didn't want to waste any more time on the Frenchman. Other questions had been stirring in her mind. "Do you want to stay here and shepherd the flock?"

Jan laughed again and pulled her closer to snuggle her back against his front. "Where'd you ever hear a phrase like that?"

"From you," she answered, trying to ignore the nuzzling he was doing to her ear. "You said you wanted to have a church and a congregation, and you wanted to 'shepherd the flock,' teaching them to be strong in the Word."

"Mmm," he began nibbling on her ear and then down her neck.

"Jan," she spoke as sharply as she could in a whisper, not wanting to wake the others who slept in the barn.

"What?"

"I'm trying to talk to you."

"Tildie, I've been talking for hours. I don't want to talk right now."

He turned her towards him and kissed her eyes, her cheeks, and her lips. She sighed and gave up trying to get any more information out of him.

❧

Jan spent most of his time talking to people while Henderson and his family repacked the repaired wagon. Henderson had bartered with some Indians for a large piece of leather formerly used for a teepee. He began cutting it to replace the burned canvas. Due to the men of the fort's quick action, not much had been damaged under the canvas. A barrel was charred, and they had to put the blankets and buffalo hides out to air. The buffalo hides were cured in what amounted to an Indian smokehouse, so they didn't smell much worse than before.

"Tildie, come with me." Jan stood at the door of the barn, holding out his hand. She took note of how serious he looked and immediately crossed over to take his hand. With a look over her shoulder to see that the children were supervised by Henderson, she went with him.

"What is it?" she asked.

They passed through the front gate of the compound, and he strolled off toward the river. When they reached the huge cottonwood tree, he sat down and pulled her down beside him.

"The men who took des Reaux to Bent's Fort just got back."

"Did they kill him?" she asked with her eyes wide. The despicable man had a talent for provoking people, and he wouldn't be smart enough not to antagonize his captors.

"No." Jan shook his head. "He got there all right. The men brought back some disturbing news."

"What?"

"Comanches are terrorizing the lower part of the Kansas territory, down through Texas and in parts of Oklahoma."

"The ranch? The settlement—Breakdon?"

"Breakdon was wiped out."

"Oh, no!" Tildie gasped. Pictures of the dusty main street, the clapboard buildings, the hitching rails flitted through her mind. Individual faces of people she had met on the rare occasions she'd gone to town sprang up. She saw the owner of the general store carrying a sack of flour to a buckboard outside the front door of his establishment. She saw three children running after a dog down the main street. She leaned against Jan and closed her eyes trying to block out those images. Those people were most probably dead. Were the men left behind on the ranch also dead? Would they ever know?

"What are we going to do?" she whispered.

"I want to go home to Ohio," he said without preamble.

"Ohio?"

"Yes." He squeezed her shoulders. "I never really wanted to settle at the homestead. I thought it best for the children, so I was willing. My real desire is to go back East. My brothers are working to help colored people get to Canada."

"Runaway slaves?" Tildie breathed the question, eyes wide with apprehension.

Jan merely nodded.

"That's very dangerous."

He nodded again.

"What do you want to do, Tildie?" he finally asked when her silence stretched too long.

Tildie leaned back and looked at him. Tears coursed down her cheeks. He reached out callused fingers and gently wiped them away.

"Yes, Jan, I want to go, too. I didn't want to go to Uncle Henry's. It doesn't hold any good memories for me, and I don't think it does for Boister, either."

"Why didn't you tell me?"

"Because I didn't think you really loved me."

His mouth fell open and for a moment, he didn't speak. "You didn't think. . .?"

She dropped her chin so she wouldn't have to look at his incredulous expression.

"*Didn't* think," he repeated. "What do you think now?"

"I thought you chose me because I was the only one around, and if more women had been available, you wouldn't have picked me."

"And what do you think now?" he repeated.

"I thought you were lonely and you liked having the children because it reminded you of your family growing up."

"And what do you think now?"

"I think I love you so much that I can't stand the thought of you not loving me."

"But you're not sure I love you." His calm voice cut through her, and she folded up as much as she could over her round belly and cried into her hands.

He put his arms around her and stroked her spine, hugging her and rocking her back and forth.

"Tildie, does God love you?"

She sniffed and nodded affirmative against his chest.

"Is He always saying 'I love you,' day in and day out, in ways you can see, hear, and feel?"

She shook her head, still not raising it from the comfortable position where she could hear his heartbeat and his voice rumble.

"But you know He loves you?"

She nodded yes again.

"Well, Matilda Borjesson, I love you. I'm only human, and I can't do near the things God has done to prove His love for you, but you're just going to have to *believe* I love you and *know* I love you." He tilted her head back and began kissing the tears away. "And when we get back to a place where there's a preacher other than myself, I'm going to marry you again. Not because we aren't married already in the eyes of God, but because you want it. And, if you want me to marry you once a year, I'll do it. If you want me to marry you once a month or once a week, I'll do it. But Tildie, my love, for all that marrying, I won't mean the vows one bit more than I do right now. The words will stay the same, but the love is going to grow."

He captured her lips then and kissed her with the commitment binding them together.

She believed.

epilogue

"Get up! Get up!" Mari bounced on the bed.

Tildie forced her eyes open. Blurry figures stood all around. Startled at the sight of so many people in her room, she reached one hand over and found Jan's place empty in the big feather bed.

Astrid, Jan's sister, stepped forward with a bundled baby in her arms. Her words came pouring forth in the same rush that characterized everything she did.

"Tomi is impatient for his breakfast. And mother is beside herself, thinking of all the details for your wedding. Jan has gone to the church to help with the decorations Aunt Julee is determined to see hung from the rafters. She's stripped the woods of ivy and woven a garland with lovely white flowers. You must see for yourself. She's been up half the night. If you don't stir yourself out of this bed, the next delegation of in-laws will be the brawny brothers."

Tildie sat up with a grin and took her squirming son. With a practiced flip of the small blanket and rearrangement of her gown, she soon had the sturdy four-month-old baby nestled against her breast. Tildie still wasn't use to this Swedish sisterhood who invaded her room without a thought. She modestly covered Tomi's bald head and her shoulder with the blanket.

Born before they reached St. Jo, Missouri, Tomi was always impatient to get done what needed to be done, including eating. If a meal were two minutes later than he expected, he would raise a holler that could be heard in three states—or that's what his proud grandpa claimed. Now that Tildie was awake, Jan's seven sisters and her own Mari and Evie crowded to find seats on every available spot on the huge bed. Talking and laughing with no sense of order to the conversation, the girls relayed every bit of information they could recall on the preparations for the wedding.

Suddenly, the room fell silent as a good-natured "Ach!" boomed from the doorway. Jan's mother entered waving a wooden spoon in one hand and flapping her long white apron much as she did when she shooed the chickens. "Out of here, out of here. Go! There's work to be done. I send one of you up to get Jan's Tildie out of bed, and here all of you are. How can she get up when you have her pinned by her sheets to the bed? Get up. Get out. Shoo."

Giggling and scuffling as they left, the sisters pushed out of the narrow door, taking Evie and Mari with them. When the last skirt had swung past the doorframe, Ingrid closed the door with a firm hand.

She came over to the bed and plopped down in one of the places just vacated by one of her frivolous daughters.

"Now." She patted Tildie's blanket covered leg. "Are you ready for this big day?"

"Yes, Mother Borjesson." Tildie grinned at the short, stout woman who'd taken to mothering her just as soon as she'd stepped through the farmhouse door.

"If your mother were here on the morning of your wedding day, she'd likely take the time to give you some Godly advice."

Tildie nodded as she efficiently shifted her son to nurse from the other side.

"I'll tell you to read Proverbs, one chapter for every day of the month. All the advice in there is what keeps a marriage together. Turning away wrath with a soft answer and such. But you notice, dear Tildie, that some of the months only have thirty days and that leaves out chapter thirty-one. I know in my bones that God has ordained a wife and mother as a special minister to His families, but I also know we women can get to thinking too highly of ourselves. On the one hand, He probably was giving us a break from stewing over just how much work it is to keep a family going, and on the other. . ." Her blue eyes twinkled with merry humor. "He didn't think we needed to hear how important we are every single month."

They both chortled over the thought.

Ingrid reached for Tomi. "Is that boy finished? I'll burp him and take him downstairs. You get ready," she ordered, already halfway to the door. "Eleven o'clock. All the family, all the neighbors, everyone from the church. We'll have the wedding of the year. It's not everyone who gets to marry one of the handsome Borjesson men twice. Hurry, girl."

A few minutes after her mother-in-law had disappeared with her baby, Tildie heard Jan's voice calling her name from outside. She went over to the open window and looked down to where he stood below.

"I thought you were hanging decorations at the church," Tildie said.

"I was. They're hung. Aunt Julee is stretched out in the back pew, sleeping. Snoring, too."

"You left her there?"

"Her house is one block from the church in town."

Jan looked perturbed.

"What's wrong?" asked Tildie.

"I'm just thanking God I married you in Colorado."

"Any particular reason?"

"Because now that you've met my family, you might have said no." He ran a hand through his hair. "Tildie?"

"Yes?"

"My mother is having the time of her life. She says I can't see you until after the wedding. Ridiculous!" He paused and looked up at her with such tenderness, she almost climbed down the trellis to give him a morning hug and kiss. He sighed. "Thanks for not getting upset."

"Jan?"

"Yes?"

"Are we going to move into the parsonage as of tonight?"

"Yes."

She grinned, knowing he would understand exactly why she wanted to be private in their own little house after two weeks in the bustling Borjesson household.

"Then I have no reason to be upset."

His answering expression of delight told her he, too, was ready to be a smaller family again. He blew her a kiss before turning to walk away.

"Meet me at the church, Matilda Harris Borjesson."

"Yes, Sir!"

A Letter To Our Readers

Dear Reader:

In order that we might better contribute to your reading enjoyment, we would appreciate your taking a few minutes to respond to the following questions. We welcome your comments and read each form and letter we receive. When completed, please return to the following:

Rebecca Germany, Fiction Editor
Heartsong Presents
PO Box 719
Uhrichsville, Ohio 44683

1. Did you enjoy reading *To See His Way?*
   ☐ Very much. I would like to see more books
      by this author!
   ☐ Moderately
      I would have enjoyed it more if _____

   _____

   _____

2. Are you a member of **Heartsong Presents**? Yes ☐ No ☐
   If no, where did you purchase this book? _____

   _____

3. How would you rate, on a scale from 1 (poor) to 5 (superior), the cover design? _____

4. On a scale from 1 (poor) to 10 (superior), please rate the following elements.

   _____ Heroine   _____ Plot

   _____ Hero   _____ Inspirational theme

   _____ Setting   _____ Secondary characters

5. These characters were special because_____

_____

_____

6. How has this book inspired your life?_____

_____

_____

7. What settings would you like to see covered in future
   Heartsong Presents books?_____

_____

_____

8. What are some inspirational themes you would like to see
   treated in future books?_____

_____

_____

9. Would you be interested in reading other **Heartsong
   Presents** titles?   Yes ❏   No ❏

10. Please check your age range:
    ❏ Under 18   ❏ 18-24   ❏ 25-34
    ❏ 35-45   ❏ 46-55   ❏ Over 55

11. How many hours per week do you read?_____

Name _____

Occupation _____

Address _____

City _____ State _____ Zip _____

> "Let your light so shine before men,
> that they may see your good works,
> and glorify your Father which is in heaven."
> MATTHEW 5:16

Introducing a brand new historical novella collection
with four female lighthouse
keepers, at four different points
of the compass in the United
States. Each woman will need to
learn to trust in God and the
guidance of His Light as they
seek to do their appointed tasks.
Salting their characters' lives with
romance, the authors bring each
of these tales to an expected yet
miraculous ending.

When Love Awaits by Lynn A. Coleman
A Beacon in the Storm by Andrea Boeshaar
Whispers Across the Blue by DiAnn Mills
A Time to Love by Sally Laity

paperback, 452 pages, 5 ³⁄₁₆" x 8"

❤ ❤ ❤ ❤ ❤ ❤ ❤ ❤ ❤ ❤ ❤ ❤ ❤ ❤

Please send me _____ copies of *Keepers of the Light*. I am enclosing $4.97 for
each. Please add $1.00 to cover postage and handling per order. OH add 6% tax.)
Send check or money order, no cash or C.O.D.s please.

Name_____

Address _____

City, State, Zip _____

To place a credit card order, call 1-800-847-8270.
Send to: Heartsong Presents Reader Service, PO Box 719, Uhrichsville, OH 44683

❤ ❤ ❤ ❤ ❤ ❤ ❤ ❤ ❤ ❤ ❤ ❤ ❤ ❤